WITHDRAWN

TACKETT
AND THE
INDIAN

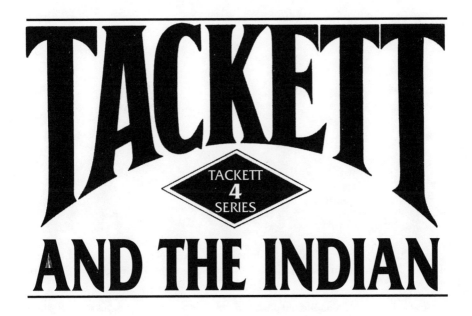

TACKETT

TACKETT
4
SERIES

AND THE INDIAN

LYN NOFZIGER

Frontier Library ■ Jameson Books, Inc.
Ottawa, Illinois

Jameson books are available at special discounts for bulk purchases for sales pro-
motions, premiums, fund raising or educational use. Special condensed or excerpted
paperback editions can also be created to customer specifications.

For information or other requests please write:

Jameson Books, Inc.
722 Columbus Street
Ottawa, Illinois 61350
815-434-7905 • FAX 815-434-7907
E-mail 72557.3635@compuserve.com

Jameson Books titles are distributed to the book trade by LPC Group, 1436 West
Randolph Street, Chicago, IL 60607. Bookstores should call 800-243-0138. Individuals
who wish to order by mail should call 800-426-1357.

Library of Congress Cataloging-in-Publication Data
Nofziger, Lyn.
    Tackett and the Indian / Lyn Nofziger.
        p.   cm. — (The Tackett series : 4)
    ISBN 0-915463-75-X (alk. paper)
    1. Indians of North America—Montana—Fiction. I. Title. II. Series:
Nofziger, Lyn.   Tackett trilogy : 4.
PS3564.034T334   1997
813'.54—dc21   97-49588
                                                                           CIP

1   2   3   4   /   99   98   97

CHAPTER 1

IF ANYONE WAS to ever ask me I'd have to tell them that jail is no fun place to be, unless you like the taste of cold and greasy food, the smell of slop buckets and the company of body lice, bed bugs, and mean drunks, none of which suit my fancy.

I've been thrown in jail three times in my twenty-nine years. The first two times—once for being drunk and disorderly and once for fighting—they turned me loose the next day. The third time—this time—it looked like I was going to stay awhile. And in a way I was glad, if only because it sure beat being lynched. And I'd come within an inch of that just the day before.

There I was on the trail to Cutbank, a little town in the northwestern part of Montana, and hoping to get there in another day or two, when I spotted a wisp of smoke coming from behind a low rise off the trail a ways. I should of minded my own business but sometimes even smart men will do dumb things and nobody ever accused me of being overly smart.

Anyways, I decided to investigate. It ran through my head that if it was a small brush fire I might be able to stomp it out before it spread. Likewise, I figured that if someone was stopping to make a noon meal he might have a spare cup of coffee, something I dearly wanted, having spilled the last of mine this morning before I had a chance to get even a little sip.

When I topped the rise I took one look at where the fire was and decided I didn't like what I saw. Not at all.

Alongside the fire was a roped and hogtied steer and standing over it with a running iron in his hand was a cowboy. He saw me about the same time I saw him. Next thing I knew, he tossed the running iron away and was reaching for the six-gun on his hip. I went out of the saddle in a hurry, shucking my own gun as I hit the ground. But what do ya know? He never took a shot at me. Instead, he sprinted for his horse, leaped into the saddle, and taken off at a gallop.

I climbed to my feet, taken the reins of Old Dobbin, my bay gelding, and walked down to the fire. The steer, a yearling, was lying on his side and I could see where the cowboy, more than likely a small rancher trying to enlarge his herd, had begun changing a Rocking W brand into something else, but he hadn't got far enough along for me to figure out what the something else was.

I fished a Barlow folding knife from my pocket and was leaning over to cut the steer loose when the sound of hoofbeats made me look up. There was four of them, all tough-looking galoots, all wearing guns and smiles that didn't seem to be smiles of welcome. Right away I knew why that rustler had taken off.

A big man with black curly hair and a reckless, uncurried look about him seemed to be the leader. He grinned down at me, then looked around at the other riders.

"Well, fellers. It looks like our friend here don't like the way we brand our cows."

"Hey, now, look," I said. "This ain't the way it seems."

"Sure it ain't," the big man drawled. "You just stumbled across this here steer, seen he was all tangled up in a rope, and was about to cut him loose."

"You got it," I said, looking around vainly for a friendly face. "I seen the smoke from the fire and come over to see what it was all about. Some feller was about to change the brand and when he seen me he taken off."

"That there's a pretty good story," the big man said, still grinning. "Only one thing wrong with it. I don't believe ya. What about you fellers?"

"Don't seem likely," one of them said.

"You got a name, Mister?" the big man asked me.

"Tackett," I said. "Del Tackett."

"Pleased to meet ya, Tackett," he said. "Me, I'm Bailey Harbor. I'm the foreman of the Rockin' W ranch. We own that there steer you found. And to show you how grateful we are to ya for findin' it we're gonna throw a party in yer honor—a necktie party."

Before I could say anything, two of the cowboys dismounted and came for me. For half a second I thought about going for my gun, but death at a young age never had no appeal for me, so I stood still whilst one of them grabbed my six-gun and stuck it in his belt.

The other one had his lasso handy and he put the noose of it over my neck and pulled it snug. He led me over to Old Dobbin and I climbed aboard, all the time thinking how once in the saddle I could yank the rope out of that cowboy's hands and be off and running.

But that was another thought I gave up on in a hurry. Old Dobbin wasn't no spring chicken any more and I'd been pushing him steady for nigh on to three weeks and he was a mite wore down. Shoot, even when he was young and frisky he couldn't of outrun a rifle bullet—and all four of those hombres was carrying rifles.

Thing that gave me hope, though, was that all four of them seemed pretty cocky. With four of them and one of me, they didn't figure I was going anywhere and they were prob'ly right, but I figured as long as I was alive I had a chance, and if one that was even half good came along I was going to take it.

We rode along for maybe a half hour. The cowboy had tied the rope around my neck to his saddle horn and he trailed along behind me to make sure I didn't try to slip free of the noose. He never figured it was necessary to tie my hands.

Pretty soon up ahead I saw some sycamore trees lining a creek. They were big trees with spreading branches that looked strong enough to hold a man, even one as big as I am, and I weigh two hundred pounds in my stocking feet.

Bailey Harbor rode up alongside of me.

"Some good lookin' trees up ahead," he said. "Since it's yer party you can take yer choice."

"Mr. Harbor," I said, "like I told you, my name is Tackett. I come from the R-Bar-R ranch down in the Arizona Territory. I'm headin' for Cutbank, up the road a ways. Got a feller there to see name of Frank Honerock, runs a little newspaper. It don't make no sense for me to be tryin' to steal one of yer cows."

"Here's what I know," he said. "The Rockin' W's been losin' cows ever since spring. I caught you with one of our cows, a fire, and a runnin' iron. I don't guess yer ever goin' to see yer friend in Cutbank."

He was riding close to me while he spoke. "That's the way it is," he said as I looked over at him. "So get used to it."

Well, what the hell, I thought, and I reached out and backhanded him across the face with all my strength, which is considerable even if I couldn't get all my weight into the blow. It caught him unawares and it knocked him half out of the saddle.

With the same motion, I yanked the noose from off my neck, leaped to the ground, grabbed Bailey Harbor by one leg, and dragged him the rest of the way off his saddle. He sprawled on the ground just as a shot hit the dirt at my feet. I looked around and seen that all three of them cowboys had their guns pointed at me.

I grinned up at them. "Figured to get my licks in afore ya hung me," I said.

Harbour staggered to his feet and brushed the dirt off the front of his shirt and licked the blood off his lips.

"Stand back, boys," he snarled. "I am going to beat the living hell out of this galoot. Then we're gonna hang him."

"Make a deal with ya," I said. "Ya whip me, ya hang me. I whip you, ya turn me loose."

His answer was to throw a sudden short left hook that caught the point of my jaw and sent me stumbling backward onto the ground. Then he came after me with both boots and caught me in the ribs with one, but I rolled away from him before he could do any serious damage and scrambled to my feet.

He was a big man, maybe not as tall as me, but every bit as broad and heavy, with a deep chest and a bull neck and short, powerful arms. Whipping him was not going to be easy, but I figured it was my only chance.

He came charging into me with both arms wide, meaning to get me in a bear hug. I ducked down low and turned a hip into him and he went flying over me and landed on his back on the ground. But he hit rolling and leaped to his feet none the worse for wear.

He came charging at me again, this time with his head low, meaning to butt me in the belly. I managed to shove him to one side as he reached for me, and when he went by I got a choke hold around his neck with my left arm and began chopping at his kidney with my right fist. I heard him grunt with pain every time I hit him and I knew he'd be seeing blood for a few days whenever he set about doing his daily duties.

But he was stronger than any ox and, even with all my weight leaning on him, he managed to rear up and throw me off. We went at it then, slugging at each other with everything we had. Neither one of us knowed much about the science of boxing and we missed as often as we landed.

It was pretty even for the first while. He cut my cheek with a looping right fist and I smashed a straight right hand into his mouth that flattened out his lips and made him spit blood. We rocked each other pretty good a time or two more but neither of us went down, mainly because we was both afraid we wouldn't be able to get up again.

After we'd been at it a while I noticed he was beginning to breathe hard through his mouth and his hands were dropping a little. He kept barreling in, though, but this one time when he come at me, I set myself and threw my weight into a right-hand punch that caught him high in the belly just below his rib cage.

He sat down suddenly, his face all red and his mouth gaping open while he fought and gasped for breath.

He finally turned over on his hands and knees and then leaned down on his forearms. Me and them cowboys just watched as he finally got his wind and staggered to his feet. He glared at me for a minute, then growled, "All right, boys, he's had his fun. Now let's hang the son of a bitch."

Just then a voice I hadn't heard before said matter-of-factly, "Ain't gonna be no hangin' today, Harbor."

When I looked around I saw a grey-haired man sitting there on a big paint horse. He wore a leather vest, and the thing I noticed about it was that there was a star pinned on the left side.

"Howdy, Sheriff," I said. "Looks like you got here just in time."

"Looks like," he said. "That was a good fight you put up there, son. Don't think anyone's ever licked old Bailey Harbor before."

He turned to Harbor. "You wanna tell me what's goin' on here?"

"He's a rustler and we're fixin' to hang him," Harbor mumbled between his mashed lips.

The sheriff turned back to me. "You a rustler, son?"

"No, sir, Sheriff. I'm the foreman of the R-Bar-R ranch down in the Arizona Territory. Headin' up the road a ways to Cutbank. Got a feller to see name of Frank Honerock. Runs a paper there."

"Honerock, huh? I've heard of him. What's this about you bein' a rustler?"

One of the cowboys broke in. "Look here, von Cart, we caught him in the act with a runnin' iron in his hand."

"It looked that way, but that ain't the way it was," I said, beginning to wonder what would happen if he believed them, and knowing it was the word of a stranger against that of four men he knew. One thing was for sure. If he turned his back and walked away from me, he wouldn't be the first western lawman to let the ranchers make their own law.

"What's yer name, Mister?" he asked.

"Tackett."

"Sackett? You say Sackett? You any kin to them Sacketts down in Colorado. I used to know a couple of 'em. Good men, too. Rode with one of 'em name of Hacken Sackett for a bit."

I shook my head. "Wisht I was, Sheriff. But it's Tackett with a T. I ain't got no kinfolk. Leastwise I don't think I have. But someone sent me a copy of the paper up there in Cutbank and it mentioned a man name of Tackett. And, well, that's why I'm headin' that way. Lookin' for kinfolk, is all."

"Don't believe him, von Cart," the cowboy said. "We caught him red-handed and we're gonna hang him."

Sheriff von Cart shook his head. "Not today you ain't. Not without Tod Websterby says so. I'll take him into town and we'll give him a fair trial and then you can hang him. In the meantime you-uns should ought to go back to the ranch. You can tell Tod I'm holdin' the man ya think is stealin' his cows."

He held up a silencing hand as a cowboy opened his mouth to argue. "Just hold on, Jake. You know Montana is due to become a state sometime this year and we don't want nothin' gettin' in the way. Word gets out that we're lynchin' people out here and Congress could dang well change its mind. No, sir, there ain't gonna be no lynchin' today.

"Now, Mister, yer my prisoner. You gonna come peaceable?"

"Peace is my middle name, Sheriff," I said, heading for Old Dobbin. "Jail sounds mighty good to me right now."

Bailey Harbor spit blood from his mouth. "You better have a quick trial, Von, 'cause I ain't gonna wait long. And neither will the boss when he hears about this."

"You'll wait as long as it takes, Harbor, and Tod Websterby knows now ain't the time to try anything funny with me," von Cart blustered.

Harbor gave a kind of derisive snort, but von Cart paid him no heed, and turned to me. "Mount up, boy. I'm taking ya in."

A half hour later we topped a low hill and looked down at a cluster of buildings nestled in a bend of the Sun River.

Sheriff von Cart waved his hand. "There she is," he said, "Kolakoka, the jewel of the Sun River Valley."

He was a man who liked to talk and he'd been talking ever since we'd ridden away from Bailey Harbor and his men. So I knew more than I'd ever wanted to know about the jewel of the Sun River Valley. Kolakoka, he'd told me, was an Indian word meaning "sparkling water."

"It ain't the river," he explained, "but a spring sitting back a ways. It has a sweet taste to it and kind of a tang. Put it in a clear glass and you can see tiny bubbles. Pretty good with whiskey."

"I ain't much for whiskey," I said. "But when I drink it I drink it straight."

"Ya oughta try our water, Mister," he said. "If ya live long enough."

"Now, look here, Sheriff," I said, "I ain't fixin' to die any time soon. I wasn't changin' the brand on that steer. Like I told Harbor, I chased off the feller who was doin' it and I was gettin' ready to cut that steer loose when they come up on me. Ya think I wouldn't of been on the lookout if I was stealin' cows?"

"We all get careless now and then," he said, but he didn't sound real sympathetic.

"I could give you the names of some folks you could wire who would stand up fer me," I said.

He chuckled. "Nearest telegraph's a hundred miles from here as the crow flies."

By this time we were coming into the outskirts of Kolakoka which reached up the hill from the Sun River. Von Cart pointed to a clump of trees off to our left that was surrounded by a barb-wire fence.

"That spring I was tellin' ya about is over in them trees. Man named Evan Peryea owns it. Says he fenced it in to keep critters out, keep 'em from muddyin' it up. But I think he's got other ideas. Like bottlin' it and sellin' it if he can figure out a way to keep the fizz in."

He went on talking but I didn't pay him much mind. Instead I was looking over the town as we trotted through it. It had one main street up a ways from the river but running even with it. And there were four cross streets, all short except for the one we came in on which crossed through the town and ran down to the river. There was no bridge here but the road kept going on the other side which meant either the river was shallow or there was a ferry, except that I didn't see one.

Kolakoka looked like most small western towns, a few business buildings, two saloons, a livery stable, a blacksmith shop, and a scattering of houses on either side of the main street but back a bit. I figured no more than a few hundred people lived there.

We rode down to the main street, turned right at the next side street and then left. The jail was just off the main street on the river side. The front of it was wood but I'd learn in a hurry that its cells had walls of stone and bars of hard steel.

There weren't many people on the street, prob'ly because there weren't many people in the town. Von Cart waved casually at a couple of them as we rode up to the jail. We dismounted and went inside, with von Cart pushing me ahead of him. It was pretty much what I'd expected. The front office had a desk, and two extra chairs. A door in the back wall opened into a hallway and there was two cells on the other side. Each cell was equipped with a bunk, a mattress and two blankets, and a slop bucket.

Von Cart took a key ring that was hanging from a nail on the wall, unlocked one of the cells, and motioned me in.

"First time in more'n a year we had someone in here who wasn't drunk or disorderly," he said, locking the door behind me.

"Sheriff, ya could do a couple of things fer me," I said.

"Yep?"

"Take good care of Old Dobbin out there. Me and him have been together for nigh on five years. I owe him."

"I'll make sure. Now what else?"

"Take good care of my six-shooter and rifle. I'll be needin' 'em."

"Sure thing," he said. He pulled a big pocket watch out of his vest pocket. "Four o'clock. I'll see that ya get some supper in a bit."

"Yer all heart, Sheriff," I said as he went out.

CHAPTER 2

Bad as it is on a freedom-loving man, sitting in jail is still better than dangling at the end of a rope, which is where I would have been if Sheriff Curt von Cart hadn't come along when he did. Because there was no doubt in my mind that Bailey Harbor had meant to hang me to a branch of one of those big sycamore trees.

A man who wore a badge on his shirt and said he was von Cart's deputy had brought me supper that first night, some slices of tough beef and beans that tasted more of grease than bean. It was cold by the time he got it to me but it wouldn't of tasted any better even when it was hot.

The deputy was a short man, a full head shorter than me, with big, calloused hands, big feet, and hardly any teeth. He was carrying a wad of snuff in his lower lip. When he came in, he set the tray on the floor outside the cell, told me to stand over against the far wall, unlocked the cell door, pushed the tray inside with his foot, slammed the door shut, and relocked it. The whole thing taken him about five seconds. It was plain he'd had a lot of practice.

He looked at me close when I came to pick up the tray. "I know you," he said. "Yer Tackett. Me, I'm Zell Botrish. I was down in El Paso when you got in that knife fight with the Mex kid. I thought he was gonna cut ya to ribbons but yer better and faster than ya look."

Instinctively my hand went up to the scar that run down my left cheek. "Better, maybe, but not faster," I said. "He cut me pretty good afore I figured him out."

"Ya didn't seem to me to be the kind to be rustlin' cows," he said.

"I ain't," I replied. "I was headed for Cutbank up near the Canadian border when Harbor and his boys grabbed me."

"Ain't the way they're tellin' it around town," he said. "They claim they caught ya red-handed. They're talkin' about bustin' ya out of here and hangin' ya and not waitin' for no trial."

"Well," I said. "I got you and the sheriff to protect me."

"Mebbe," he said, "But don't count on it. Tod Websterby comes to town with the rest of his men and begins to stir up the townsfolk agin ya, von Cart'll find it best to be out of town. He's Websterby's man and he only kept Harbor from hangin' ya because Websterby hadn't told him no different. He'll be gone all right."

"And you, too," I said bitterly.

He nodded and spit a gob of tobacco juice on the floor. "And me, too."

"I guess it don't make much difference," I said. "It's my word against four of them. Why don't we have a trial and get it over with?"

"Got a circuit judge in these parts," he said. "He ain't due until next week. I wouldn't bet much that you'll last until then." He rolled himself a cigarette and puffed on it silently whilst I ate, then he backed me up against the far wall again, taken the tray, and left, turning around just long enough to say, "Don't hold it against von Cart. He ain't a bad man. Weak, maybe, but not bad. Thing is, nobody in this neck of the woods can stand up against old Tod Websterby."

It was getting dark outside by the time he left and it was even darker inside. I went back and sat on the edge of my bunk, contemplatin' the injustices of the world I lived in and wishin' I'd been smart enough to stay back in Arizona where I belonged.

When I got tired of that, I reached down and pulled up my left pant leg and patted the handle of the knife that nestled in a thin case strapped to my left leg. It was my ace in the hole. It had saved my life on more than one occasion and had cost one man his. Not many folks knew about it and it wasn't something I ever mentioned.

I took it out and felt of it. It was razor sharp and came to a needle point. I'd shaved with it more than once. Question was, would I live to shave with it again?

Breakfast in the morning was better than supper. It was flapjacks and bacon, and whoever had put it together had included butter and a small pot of honey. A slim young woman who looked to be part Indian, what with her straight black hair and round face, carried it in with Botrish right behind her. He backed me against the wall again, unlocked the cell door, and let her in.

"Just set it anywhere, Miss," I said politely.

"This is my daughter, Clara," Botrish said. "She's workin' over at the cafe, temporary-like. Her ma is a full-blooded Sioux. She's got a couple of cousins who helped scalp General Custer."

"Pleased to meet ya, Miss Botrish," I said.

She smiled, showing even white teeth. "Don't pay any mind to my father. My mother says none of the warriors in our family were anywhere near that battle."

"Dang it, Clara," Botrish complained. "There ya go again, ruinin' a good story."

"I've got to get back to the restaurant," she said. "Daddy, you bring the tray when he's through eating."

"Seems like a nice girl," I said after she left.

Botrish grinned proudly, showing one tooth and lots of gum. "Smart, too. Went to school over in Butte. Gonna be a teacher next fall over there.

"By the way, rumor is Websterby's comin' to town tomorrow with some of his men. 'Pears to me they're lookin' for trouble."

"What're you gonna do?" I asked.

"Sheriff had business down the road a ways. He left early this mornin'. If he ain't back by the time Websterby comes to town, I'll go look for him. Prob'ly won't make it back in time to do much. Bury ya, maybe." He spat another wad of tobacco juice on the floor and turned to go.

"Botrish," I said. "I need a favor first. I need to write a letter to folks at the R-Bar-R ranch down in Arizona. Can ya get me a pencil and paper?"

"I'll send Clara over with some when she brings yer noon meal," he said.

It was early afternoon before Clara arrived with a trayful of food and a pencil and a writing tablet. She set the tray on the floor and went and got the key to the cell.

"Mr. Tackett would you please go stand next to the wall, facing it?" she asked politely.

"Aw, Miss Clara," I said. "I ain't gonna bother ya. You got my word on that."

"Mr. Tackett, either you do what I say or I will leave, taking your meal and the pencil and paper with me."

I went and stood close to the wall, facing it. "Yer a hard woman, Miss Clara," I said.

"Careful, too," she said, unlocking the cell door and pushing the tray in with her foot.

She smiled at me as I came to get it, and her black eyes kind of sparkled. "I wouldn't of bothered ya none, Miss Clara," I said.

"Mr. Tackett," she said, "I would like to believe you, but I always remember what my grandfather, who was an important man in our tribe, used to say: 'White man speak with forked tongue.'"

I shrugged. "Well, anyway, thanks for bringin' the pencil and paper. When I'm finished maybe you could mail it fer me."

"I would be glad to, Mr. Tackett," she said.

The food wasn't too bad, beans and something that tasted like venison stew and a big chunk of bread. There was also a steaming cup of coffee that was hot and black and tasted good. After I finished eating I set the tray over by the cell door and went to writing.

Now I don't write very good and I read kind of slow. Up to a year ago it was about all I could do to write my own name and whilst I could read printing a little bit I had real trouble trying to make out handwriting. I got lucky, though. A young woman name of Liddy Doyle taken it on herself to teach me how to read and also how to write by hand. After that I'd gone back to the R-Bar-R there on the Arizona-New Mexico border where I'd been foreman before and where Esmeralda Rankin, who owned the ranch, was waiting for me. Her and me were fixing to get married, but I'd put it off a while because of getting the word that there was a Tackett up near Cutbank.

Now I hadn't never heard of no Tacketts except me and Ma and I'd always figured I was a orphan. I'd grown up in the high mountains of the Sierra Nevada where Ma had scrabbled out a living panning for gold. She was a widow woman who'd lost her husband in the War Between the States and had fled to the mountains after she killed a man in Carson City who was bothering her.

Ma was from Philadelphia, but her husband, Bennett William Tackett, who Ma called Ben Bill, was a Virginian who was a lieutenant in the army. When the war broke out he sided with the South and joined the Confederate army. He left Ma with her folks in Philadelphia, her in a family way with her first and it turned out only child—me. Then Ma's folks went and died during the war leaving her with a baby and no money. Ma never heard from Ben Bill after he left to fight for the South, and he never came home after the war.

When Ma died the only thing she left behind was a diary, and after I learned to read, it was from it that I learned the little I knew about my Pa.

I'd never really thought about the possibility of having other kinfolk, although I'd often wished I had some. Whenever someone mistakenly called me "Sackett," which happened from time to time, a great feeling of loneliness would come over me. There were, I knew, Sacketts scattered all through the West and they were all kinfolk, brothers, cousins, and the like, and whenever one got in trouble the others always seemed to come a-running.

Me, I didn't have anyone to come to my aid, not really. Oh, I had friends that a time or two had been there in a pinch, but it wasn't the same. There wasn't blood that we shared, and that made it different.

It turned out that Esmeralda's father, Colonel Reagan Rankin, used to be a close friend of this Frank Honerock feller who owned a little newspaper in Cutbank, and Esmeralda had stayed in touch with him after her father was killed. In one of her letters to him, she mentioned me and he wrote back saying there was an old rancher up in his neck of the woods named Tackett who was a friend of his, but was pretty much a hermit and never came to town much. He didn't know much about him, only that he'd fought in the War Between the States. He was curious to know, was I any kin?

I told Esme that I didn't think I had any kin in Montana or anywhere else and I tried to shake it from my mind, but I couldn't. Was there a chance that the Tackett up there in Cutbank would be Ben Bill Tackett, Lt. Bennett William Tackett, late of the Confederate army? If he was, then that was my Pa up there, a man I'd never known, a man I thought was killed in the war. And if it *was* my Pa why had he deserted Ma? And if he wasn't, was he kinfolk at all, an uncle, a cousin, someone who shared my blood and my ancestors? The questions wouldn't go away, and finally I decided I would never rest easy 'til I had some answers.

Our wedding was just a month off when I made up my mind.

"Esme," I said one evening, after we'd talked awhile. "I got to go. I just got to."

Tears welled up in her dark eyes, but she taken my hand and said, "I know, Del. I know. I would feel the same way. But I don't want to lose you again. Let's get married right away and then I know you'll come back to me."

"I've always come back, Esme," I said. "And I always will. There ain't no woman but you. And there never will be. But it would be wrong to marry you now. I'll try to be back by fall roundup time and we'll be married then, I promise you."

"You're a stubborn man, Del Tackett," she said, "and you'll never change. But I love you and that will never change, either. So go, but hurry and come back as soon as you can. I'll be waiting."

A great yearning welled up in me then, and I taken her in my arms, longing for the day that I would take her to our bed. I kissed her hard and we held each other tight for a minute, then she pulled back.

"Go," she whispered. "But come back. Please, please, come back."

"I'll be back" I said hoarsely, turning to go. "Ain't nothin' can stop me."

Those words came back to me strong as I sat on the edge of that jail cell bunk, trying to think up the words that would tell Esme that I wouldn't be coming back after all.

I must of sat there for an hour, trying to think up what to say,. And all of a sudden I was angry, mad clean through. I hadn't committed no crime, regardless of what it looked like. Bailey Harbor and his men just thought it would be fun to hang someone. I threw the tablet on the floor and stood up. The gang from the Rocking W was going to play hell if they tried to hang me. Oh, they might do it all right, but they weren't going to have it easy. Somebody besides me was going to get hurt when they tried it. I reached down and patted the knife strapped to my leg. If Tod Websterby and his men were coming to town tomorrow, I'd better think about getting out of here tonight.

I went over to the cell window and rattled the bars. Only thing was, they wouldn't rattle. They were set solid and deep in the rock wall of the jail. I looked at the ceiling. It was heavy planks and it was ten feet above the floor. Even standing on the bunk, I couldn't get enough leverage to see if I could push one loose.

I checked the bars on the front of the cell. They wouldn't budge. I looked at the lock, but I wasn't no locksmith and there wasn't a key in sight. The hinges on the cell door were fastened with heavy rivets. I went back and looked at the window bars again with the idea of digging them out with the point of my knife. Give me a month undisturbed and a new knife every day and it might work.

It was beginning to look like my only chance was to trick Zell Botrish or Clara into coming close enough so's I could get the key, even if it meant hurting one of them, which I didn't want to do.

It was just beginning to get dark when the door from the front of the jail opened and Clara Botrish came into the hallway, closing the door behind her. She came up to the bars.

"Mr. Tackett," she said in a low, urgent voice, "I need to talk to you."

I approached her warily. "What is it?"

"Tod Websterby and the men from the Rocking W are in town and they're talking about lynching you tonight."

"How do ya know?"

"I overheard two of them talking in the cafe. They think I'm an Indian so they didn't pay any attention to me. If they lynch you, Mr. Tackett, it will be the sheriff's fault and my father's fault and my fault, too. I don't know if you're guilty or not but I can't let them hang you without a trial."

"Clara," I said. "I'm innocent. You got to believe that."

"It doesn't matter," she said frantically. "I'm going to turn you loose, but you're going to have to hit me and tie me up so it looks like you escaped."

She shoved the key into the lock, turned it, and swung the door open. "Hit me," she commanded. "Tear my dress. Make it look real."

"I can't do that, Miss Clara," I said.

"Do it," she demanded. "Here, I'll rip my dress."

"No need to do that," Zell Botrish said as the door to the outer office swung open again. He was standing there with a .45 colt six-shooter that looked as big as a cannon in his hand.

For an instant I thought about grabbing his daughter and using her as a shield. But I couldn't do that either.

Clara swung around at the sound of her father's voice. "Father!" she exclaimed. "What are you doing here? You said you were going after the sheriff."

"I thought about it," he said. "But it weren't right and I knowed it. So I come back to defend my prisoner."

"Don't be a fool, Botrish," I said. "Ya can't stand against that bunch. By the time they get around to comin' for me, they'll have half the men in town with 'em, all yellin' for a piece of my hide. They'll gun ya down and hang me before midnight and ya know it."

"Yer right," he said grimly, clamping his thin lips together. "Come on, Clara. Ain't no use you and me gettin' in the middle of this thing. They're gonna hang Tackett anyways, and there ain't nothin' we can do about it."

"Father!" she hissed. "You go if you wish. But if you make Mr. Tackett go back in that cell, I'm going with him. We just can't let them hang him."

"You'd do that for a feller ya hardly know?" Botrish asked in wonderment.

"I'd do it for another human being," she said. "You call us Indians savages, but nobody is as savage as the white man. You sent me to the white man's schools to learn and to be civilized and what I learned is that the white man isn't any more civilized than the red man.

"Go ahead and leave, Father, if you must. But I'm staying."

"They'll kill ya, daughter," he argued frantically. "They'll rape ya and torture ya and then they'll kill ya. Yer just a injun to them. And with white men like Websterby and Harbor, anything goes when yer dealin' with injuns."

"I'm staying," she said. "You go on and go."

He looked at us both uncertainly, wavering, then suddenly he made up his mind, shoved his hogleg back into its holster, and spat a large gob of tobacco juice on the floor.

"You win," he said to his daughter. "Come on, Tackett. Let's get yer guns and we'll figure out how we get out of here."

In the front office I strapped on my gunbelt and checked my old Colt Peacemaker to be sure it was loaded and in working order. I took my rifle from where it was standing in the corner and made sure it was loaded, too.

"Where's the stable?" I asked.

"North end of town, west side of the road," Botrish replied.

"Best thing to do," I said. "Is for you and Clara to slip out of here. Clara, you go back to the restaurant and try to act natural. Zell, you go on over to the saloon so's they'll see ya and maybe that'll slow 'em down."

He shook his head. "It won't work. They find yer gone, they'll blame me and hang me in yer place. If we're bustin' ya out of here, we're goin', too. We ain't got no choice."

"Where'll ya go?" I asked.

"Her Ma's tribe is camped up north of here a ways. We'll try to make it to them."

"We'll go together." I said. "I'm headin' north for Cutbank, anyways. And three's better'n two. You two go now and get yer horses. Soon as it gets a little darker, I'll duck out of here and head for the livery stable. I'll meet ya there in about thirty minutes. If anything goes wrong you'll hear the noise. In that case you take off and I'll try to catch up."

Botrish looked up at me for a moment, then stuck out his hand. "Luck, Boy," he said.

"And to you, too," I said. "And ... thanks. I won't forget."

They turned to go, but Clara stopped and turned back around. She stepped up close to me and standing on her tiptoes she kissed me on the cheek.

"All white men aren't savages," she whispered.

CHAPTER 3

I WATCHED THEM go in wonderment. I hardly knew them and yet they were willing to risk their lives to save mine. It would of been easy enough for them to look the other way. No one would of given it a second thought. I was a stranger in a strange land, and if some of the locals took it in their heads to lynch me no one would care and I'd soon be forgotten. And down on the R-Bar-R, Esme Rankin would wait a while and wonder and maybe weep a little, but life would go on and one day someone else would come along to fill the empty spot I left in her life.

One thing for sure, I owed Zell Botrish and his daughter more than I could ever repay. But there was one thing I could do as part payment: I could do my best to make sure they reached Clara's mother's people safely.

After they'd gone I went over to the sheriff's desk and rummaged around looking for extra cartridges. I found a boxful, stuffed them in my pocket, and was about to head outside when the door opened and a tow-headed cowboy stepped in.

"Botrish around?" he asked.

"Sorry, he ain't," I said. "He asked me to kind of look after things 'til he got back."

"Harbor told me to come tell him he better go find the sheriff. The old man's gettin' in a hurry to get this over with, so as soon as Botrish comes back tell him to take off."

"I'll tell him," I said.

I waited 'til I was sure he was gone and went outside. It was dusk and lights were beginning to go on around town. There wasn't anyone on the street. Those who wanted to lynch me were whooping it up in one of Kolakoka's two saloons and the rest of the townsfolk had retreated to their homes.

I walked up the street real casual, doing my best to look like I didn't have a care in the world, turned up the main road out of town—the road me and the sheriff had ridden in on the day before—and headed for the livery stable. A skinny kid who looked about sixteen and in need of a bath was standing by the stable door talking to Zell and Clara Botrish when I came up. He was pimply faced and a cigarette dangled from his loose lips. He wore a Colt .45 slung low on his right hip, like he wanted folks to know how tough he was.

"Sheriff dropped a bay gelding off here yesterday. I come to get it," I said.

The kid tossed his cigarette on the ground and looked questioningly at Botrish.

"It's all right," Botrish said.

"The hell it is," the kid yelled and dived for his gun. Before his hand even touched the gun butt, Botrish reached out a long arm and grabbed the boy by the upper arm and squeezed. The kid let out a yelp of pain and struggled to get loose but Botrish held on tight and pulled him over close.

"I said it's all right," he said softly.

"Yer hurtin' me," the kid whispered.

"Not as much as I will if ya don't do what yer told," Botrish said, still talking in a low tone. "Now son, you reach down and unbuckle that gunbelt unless you want me to hurt ya real bad."

The kid's face had turned white from pain and he was doing his best not to cry out. He reached down with his left hand, unbuckled the gun belt, and let it drop to the ground. Botrish let him go with a shove.

The kid looked at him. "He's a rustler," he whispered. "They're gonna hang him. Why are ya lettin' him go?"

Botrish spat tobacco juice in the dirt at the kid's feet.

"Son," he said, "Montana's due to become a state this year. Bein' a state means havin' law and order and that means we don't hang folks without a trial. One of these days, son, it wouldn't surprise me if most folks quit carrying guns around with 'em."

He turned to me. "You better find some rope so's we can tie this kid up. Don't need him runnin' to Websterby. It's a long way to Helena and we need all the start we kin get."

I found some rope in the back of the stable and in no time at all we had him tied tight. Botrish took the kid's dirty bandana and used it for a gag. In the meantime I found Old Dobbin. He reached out and nuzzled me and I knowed he was glad to see me. It taken just a minute for me to saddle him and lead him out. We all three swung into our saddles and taken off at a brisk trot. Somewhere Clara had changed into jeans and was riding astride her little palomino like a man.

With Botrish leading the way and me bringing up the rear we went down the road, crossed the main street, headed for the Sun River, and splashed across it. After a little bit he swung on to a trail heading due north.

I rode up alongside of him. "Helena's southeast of here and yer headin' north."

He chuckled. "I thought maybe the kid would tell 'em we're headed for Helena," he said. "But like I told ya back at the jail, we're headin' north to take up with Clara's mother's people. We should get there sometime tomorrow."

We rode 'til the moon was high in the sky, sometimes at a trot, other times slowing to a walk. Finally Botrish turned off of the trail like he knowed where he was going. We weaved in and out amongst scattered trees and rocks for a bit. When he finally stopped we were a good half mile off the trail.

"We'll camp here," he said. "No fire tonight but maybe we can have a little one in the mornin' so's we can have coffee and a bite to eat."

We dismounted and unsaddled the horses. I taken some handfuls of dried grass and rubbed Old Dobbin down and the other two did the same to their horses.

"I ain't expectin' trouble," Botrish said as we were spreading out our bedrolls. "But it don't do to take chances. I'll take the first watch.

Clara can take the second and you take the third. Be a good idea to wake us up at first light. We got a ways to go yet."

The moon was down when Clara shook me out of a deep, dreamless sleep.

"Everything is quiet, Mr. Tackett. You were sleeping so hard I let you sleep for an extra hour. You must not have had any sleep in jail, knowing there were men out there who planned to hang you."

I rubbed the sleep from my eyes and reached for my boots. "That was mighty thoughtful of you, Miss Botrish. I was kind of wore out."

With no moon it was pitch dark back among the rocks and trees and when I heard the noise back toward the trail we'd come from I was comforted by knowing that, if anyone was there, he or they couldn't see us any more than I could see them. Still, I wondered who would be about this hour of the night and why would they be headed toward us, us being way off the beaten track. I strained to hear the noise again and in a moment it came, the click of a horseshoe against rock. I knowed then it wasn't no wild animal; it was someone on horseback. I eased over to where Botrish was sleeping and shook him awake. "Don't make no noise," I said. "Someone's comin'."

He sat up and stretched and yawned. "Don't surprise me none," he said. "I expected him afore now."

"Expected who?" I asked.

"Pick Boone. He was to come along as soon as he saw which way Websterby and his men were headed. He knows this country like the back of his hand and I told him where we'd be spendin' the night."

"Pick Boone?" I said.

"Picken Boone. He's a old trapper and buffalo hunter. Him and me we wintered together a time or two afore the country got civilized. The rheumatism's got him these days so he pretty much stays in town. But he can still move around if he has to."

"Call him in then," I said.

"He'll make hisself known—if it's him," Botrish said. "If it ain't, we'll know that soon enough, too."

A moment later there was a louder sound of a moving horse and against the horizon I could see the outline of horse and rider coming toward us.

A low voice called, "Ho, the camp."

"Light and set, Pick," Botrish said in a conversational tone.

"Thought ya might be here somewheres," Picken Boone said. He heaved a sigh and swung stiffly from his horse. "Danged rheumatiz," he grunted, tethering his horse to a sapling. "You all can come out now."

Botrish and his daughter moved out into the small open space. I stayed behind the rock I'd chosen and said nothing.

Botrish chuckled. "Tackett's here somewheres, but he's a suspicious galoot. Can't say as how I blame him none. Which way'd Websterby head, Pick?"

"Split his men," Boone said. "Took half of 'em south toward Helena because of what the kid at the livery stable told 'em. But Websterby's a pretty canny feller. Said maybe you was tryin' to trick him, so he had Bailey Harbor take the other half and head north toward Cutbank on account of that's where Tackett told 'em he was headin'. They'll prob'ly be ahead of ya by the time ya hit the main trail."

He stopped and spat, then continued. "If I was ol' Bailey, ya know what I'd do? I'd leave me a couple of men back where this trail joins the main one and have 'em wait and see who comes along. Anyone comin' from this direction 'ud be a sittin' duck fer a man with a rifle."

"Nobody followin' ya?" Botrish asked.

"Nary a soul. I'd know if there was."

I stepped out from behind my rock. "If yer sure of that we might as well have some coffee."

"Could use some," Boone said wearily, sitting down and leaning his back against a rock.

The first light was beginning to show above the mountains to the east of us and by it Clara and I found a few dry sticks. In a minute we had a small fire going and Botrish had gotten out a coffee pot, filled it with water from his canteen and dumped in a handful of coffee.

By the light of the fire I got a look at Boone. He was a tall, spare old man with a white beard and long, white hair. He sat there trying to rub the pain and stiffness out of his rheumatic knee joints with his gnarled rheumatic fingers.

"It's hell to get old," he grumbled. "Can't hardly walk, can't hardly use a gun no more. Takes forever to pee. Oops! Sorry, Clara. Didn't mean to say that."

Clara looked up from where she was shaving strips of bacon into a frying pan and smiled at him. "That's all right, Uncle Pick. I'm not one of those fancy town ladies. You can say whatever you want."

"Yer better'n any lady," Boone said. "Ol' Zell here is a mighty lucky man."

"Pick," I said. "Is there another trail we can take?"

He thought for a moment and finally said, "A couple of miles up the trail yer on is a old injun trail that might do the trick. Ya gotta look hard to spot it, but Zell oughta remember it. We been over it a time or two. Gets a little lighter'n I'll draw ya a map."

"Ya ain't coming along?" Botrish asked.

Boone shook his head. "Gettin' too old for this sort of thing. 'Sides, my woman's waitin' fer me back in town."

"No need to draw a map," Botrish said. "I recollect where it is."

Boone swallowed the last of his coffee and rose painfully to his feet. "Be gettin'," he said, heading for his horse.

"I'd forgot all about that old injun trail," Botrish said as we went about breaking camp. "It'll cross the river and the main trail this side of where we would of crossed 'em. Then it'll go through a low pass and head north on the other side of the mountains from the main trail. Soon as we get through the pass, though, we can leave the trail and head about due north to Cutbank."

"Thought ya was gonna hole up with yer wife's people," I said.

"Might, if we run across 'em, but me and Clara talked a little after we left ya yesterday and decided we'd like to trail along with ya, if you'll have us. Neither one of us wants to go back to livin' in a tepee, and Clara don't fancy the idea of windin' up as some buck's squaw."

"How far to Cutbank, you reckon?"

"Sixty, seventy miles. Two days ride, maybe three, dependin' on how hard we push it."

"Anything between here an' there?"

"Nothin' much. No towns. A few scattered ranches and mines and mebbe some injuns. But they're peaceable now, or was the last I heard."

The sun wasn't yet up when we reached the trail we'd left the night before and were heading north. After we'd rode a bit longer Botrish suddenly turned off, rode a few yards, and reined in.

"This is it," he said. "Look sharp and you can see traces of it. It's a old trail, older'n the Sioux. Matter of fact, they kind of shied aways from it. Called it a ghost trail."

"I can see why," I said. "Ya dang near have to be a ghost to foller it. You lead the way, Botrish."

Botrish taken off threading his way through trees and rocks for about a mile until we came to the Sun River. It was wide here but shallow and we splashed through it without any trouble. On the far bank Botrish scouted around and found where the trail picked up.

"The main trail ain't too far away," he said as Clara and me rode up to where he was waiting. "You and Clara wait here. I'm gonna scout up ahead. Don't wanta run into anyone unexpected-like."

He dismounted, traded his boots for a pair of moccasins, and taken off through the woods.

"Pretty spry old man," I said to Clara. "Looks to know the woods, too."

"Father is better in the woods than any Indian," she replied. "I should know. And he loves them. If it weren't for me, he'd probably still be spending his life hunting and trapping."

"Ain't no life for a young woman," I said.

"That's what he thinks, too. I spent a lot of my growing up years in the woods with him and I can use a rifle almost as well as he can. He tried to teach me all the woods lore he knows and he likes to brag that I was an apt pupil.

"But still, he's right. I would like to see a little more of civilization and have some of the nicer things in life. Someday, if I can save up enough money teaching, I want to go to San Francisco or St. Louis or even Philadelphia."

Her black eyes sparkled as she talked and I could see that the thought excited her. She was a pretty young woman, almost as dark as an Indian and with Indian features softened by the white man's blood. Her hair, like an Indian's, was black and straight.

"My Ma was from Philadelphia," I said, without thinking.

"Oh," she said. "You must tell me about all about it."

"We left there when I was a baby," I said. "I growed up in the high mountains of California."

"You've been to San Francisco, then?"

I shook my head. "Was to Sacramento once."

After that we just sat there on our horses, not talking, her with her dreams and me with my memories. Pretty soon I dismounted and walked down to the river's edge. It was calm and peaceful there, like all my troubles were a million miles away. I sat down and leaned back against the trunk of a large tree and watched the river flow by. It reminded me of my life, just flowing aimless, without a care, without a purpose.

I must of dozed off because the next think I knew someone kicked me in the ribs with the point of his boot. I woke up with a start and there was that pimply-faced kid from the livery stable. He was standing off to one side a few feet and he had his gun in his hand and it was pointed at me.

"I gotcha this time, Mr. Rustler," he said, his voice high-pitched with excitement. "You move and I'll kill ya, sure."

"Ya shouldn't of kicked me, kid," I said, rubbing my side and feeling stupid for letting a boy get the drop on me.

"That ain't nothin' compared to what old Tod Websterby is gonna do to ya," he sneered.

"I don't get it, kid," I said. "What's in it fer you? Why're you so all-fired eager to see me hang?"

"You don't know?" he said. "Well, I got me a couple of reasons. Fer one, Mr. Websterby offered a hunderd dollar reward fer anyone who caught ya. Fer another, this'll make me a big man in

Kolakoka and then old Evan Peryea's girl won't high-hat me no more."

I just looked at him. This pimply-faced kid was willing to see me hang for a hundred dollars and a smile from some girl. That kind of got me.

The way I was sitting, there was no way I could get at my gun but I knowed one thing for sure—that kid wasn't going to take me back to Kolakoka alive. I didn't want to die at all, but I figured I'd a sight rather die by a bullet than by hanging. Now, if I could just get at my knife.

"All right, Mister, get up real careful," the kid ordered, like he was reading my mind, "and don't let yer hand get anywheres near yer gun."

Careful, I climbed to my feet, holding my hands well away from my sides.

"Now reach down with yer left hand and unbuckle yer gun belt and let her fall."

I did as I was told.

"Now turn around."

Here it comes, I thought. The kid's gonna bash me so's he can tie me up without any trouble. I turned and braced myself for a blow, all the time straining to hear him approach, figuring maybe I could turn as he was swinging his gun and get a-hold of him afore he could bring it down and level it at me.

"Drop your gun, Willie. I've got you dead center in my sights."

The voice was Clara's.

"Now!" she snapped.

I heard a sound like something hitting the ground.

"All right, Mr. Tackett. You can turn around," she said.

I turned and looked at the kid. He looked like he was going to cry from either frustration or anger or maybe both. I picked up my gun belt and buckled it on.

"Back up, Willie," Clara ordered. "Please get his gun, Mr. Tackett."

I picked up Willie's gun and Clara stepped out from behind the bushes.

Willie looked at her in surprise. "Where's yer gun?"

Clara gave a low laugh. "Back on my horse," she said. "I didn't think I had time to go get it."

Willie stared at Clara and swore a long string of cuss words. "Tricked," he said, finally. "And by a damn girl."

"Willie," I said, "I don't wanta hear no more cussin' from ya in front of a lady. Ya do and I might have to turn ya over my knee and spank ya."

CHAPTER 4

IT TAKEN ME a while to figure out what to do with Willie. He wasn't much more than a boy and I didn't want to hurt him. On the other hand, I didn't want him hurting me, either, and there wasn't no doubt that he knew how to use that six-gun he'd been carrying. There wasn't no way I was going to turn him loose. I figured if I tied him to a tree he might starve to death before anyone found him. And I didn't want to take him with us. He'd just be in the way.

Finally it come to me.

"Willie," I said, "where's yer horse?"

"Go to hell," he spat, toughlike.

"You'll walk without him," I said. "Barefoot."

He thought that over for a bit, then glumly told me where the horse was. I left Clara to watch him whilst I fetched it. Clara had already tied his hands whilst I held a gun on him, and then she'd gone and got her own horse and the rifle it was carrying in a boot attached to the saddle.

"Horse know the way home, Willie?" I asked.

He nodded, sullen and sore.

He was sitting on the ground, so I went over and pulled him to his feet by his coat collar. Then, still holding on to the collar, I reached down and grabbed the seat of his pants and with a mighty heave flang him into the saddle. I tied his hands to the saddle horn, taken the reins, and led the horse with him on it back across the Sun River. I pointed the horse down the trail and gave him a swat on the flank with the flat of my hand. He started off at a trot and in a minute was out of sight around a bend in the trail.

I splashed Old Dobbin back across the Sun to where Clara was waiting.

"Do you think he'll be all right?" she asked, just a touch of concern in her voice.

"Danged if I know," I said. "But at least he ain't dead yet. And neither am I. Thanks to you," I added.

"I don't think we've seen the last of him," she said. "He think's he's a gunman and he's bound and determined to prove it."

"Boothills all over the West are filled with young fellers like him, fellers who thought they were gunfighters," I said. "Yer daddy could tell ya that."

About that time her daddy broke through the trees and headed to where we were sitting, mostly hidden in the shadow of a big, moss-covered rock. We'd tethered Old Dobbin and Clara's palomino mare that she called Apples, behind the rock.

"Light and set," I invited as he rode up.

He swung off his horse, spat out a wad of tobacco juice, and squatted down facing us. He fished a sack of Bull Durham from his pocket, got out a piece of paper, and rolled a cigarette. He lit it, inhaled deeply, and blew it all out.

"Trail's clear," he said. "I scouted north about a mile to where the trail we took last night crosses the Sun and joins up with the main road. And sure enough, ol' Websterby left hisself a couple of men hidin' in the bushes on the off chance we might come along."

"Instead," he said, "this is what we're gonna do."

He cleared a piece of ground and taken a twig and drew a crude map in the dirt. He showed the river and our trail crossing it and then crossing the main north-south trail that I'd figured to take on to Cutbank. That trail followed the river a ways but then branched off to head due north toward Fort Browning. From there another road went almost due east to Cutbank.

Using the twig, Botrish showed our trail heading north on the far side of a range of hills that bordered the main trail. "About here," he said, pointing to a spot about twenty miles north of where we were sitting, "we leave the trail and cut straight across country to Cutbank.

My own feelin' is that when Websterby reaches the fort and finds you ain't been there, he'll turn around and go home. That's a mean old man and he'd of hung you just for the fun of it—me, too, for gettin' in his way—but I don't see him chasin' off to Cutbank without knowin' yer there."

"Thing I still don't understand," I said, "is why the sheriff didn't let Bailey Harbor hang me right away instead of waitin' for Websterby to do it."

"Easy answer to that," Botrish said. "Ol' Von wants to run for the legislature as soon as Montana becomes a state, so he figured he had to take ya to jail to show he's a big law an' order man. He don't mind buckin' Harbor to do that, but he ain't about to buck Harbor's boss, not when he's the big injun in this part of the country."

"I guess that don't surprise me none," I said. "I had me a friend down on the border name of Herb Bushwalker. He had kinfolk was in politics and he said they'd start out meanin' well and wind up doin' anything they had to do to get elected. I guess statehood'll bring civilization but there's gonna be a lot of bad comes along with the good."

Botrish shrugged. "Mebbe the injun way is better. Who knows?"

He rose to his feet and headed for his horse. "Time to be movin' along."

He led the way through scattered trees and rocks along what sometimes seemed like a game trail and other times just wasn't there at all. After some distance we broke out into the open and there in front of us was the main north-south road, looking more like a trail than a road, barely wide enough for a buckboard or a stagecoach, and with no sign that either one had been along any time in the recent past.

Botrish pulled up and waited for me and Clara to join him. When we did, I could see he was chuckling.

"Got me an idee," he said, grinning his near-toothless grin. "You and Clara cross the trail and wait over there in the trees. I'll be back afore long."

He taken off at a trot, heading north.

I looked at Clara but she just shook her head. "Don't ask me," she said. "You know the white man. He's notional."

We crossed the trail and waited in the dark shadow of a large rock. In a little while I heard the sound of horses approaching from the north. We eased our own horses back closer to the rock and waited. It wasn't but a minute before Zell Botrish hove into view leading two saddled horses.

I rode out into the open and waved at him. In a minute he came riding up wearing the same grin he'd ridden away with.

"Websterby's boys have got a long walk ahead of 'em," he chuckled.

"They hang ya for stealin' horses," I said.

"I didn't steal 'em," he said. "They wasn't tied tight and they just wandered away. Wouldn't be surprised if they didn't head fer home."

He tossed the reins over their heads and spanked each one on the flank. They taken off at a trot down the trail toward Kolakoka.

"Time we was gettin'," he said, leading off again at an easy canter.

Our way led east through a gap in the hills and then took a turn to the north alongside them. We'd rode till past noon when Botrish pulled up again. He pointed northeast down along a small creek.

"That's likely Clara's people," he said.

I looked and saw a thin plume of smoke lifting through the trees.

"Figured they'd be camped up here somewheres," he said.

"Yer Ma down there?" I asked Clara.

She shook her head. "Mother is long dead. But if that's my people my grandfather and an uncle will be with them."

"We'll spend the night with 'em," Botrish said. "They're good people."

"Supposin' it ain't them?" I said.

"Who else would it be?" Botrish snapped.

"Almost anyone. Other injuns, trappers. Websterby's men, mebbe," I replied.

"Not likely them," Botrish said. "Main trail's on the other side of the hills from them."

"Let's go see," I said, nudging Old Dobbin gently with my spurs.

We followed the trail alongside the mountain, keeping the smoke in sight, for another hour. Then Botrish led us down off the mountain and onto brush-covered flatland. Ahead of us less than a mile away was a large stand of mixed pine and fir trees.

"I know this place," Botrish said as I rode along beside him. "Clara's people have camped here before. There's a good spring back in there and there's game around, or at least there was a few years back."

I reined in Old Dobbin and hooked a leg around the saddle horn whilst I got out the makings and rolled myself a cigarette. I'm not much of a smoker, but now and then tobacco tastes good when I just want to set and contemplate.

"Tell ya what," I said. "You and Clara go on in if ya want. Me, I wanta look around a mite. Sometimes things ain't what they seem."

"Skittish, ain't ya?" Botrish said.

"Just tryin' to stay alive," I said. "You two go on in if ya want to. I'll catch up to ya after a bit."

They headed off toward the woods and I watched them go, feeling a little foolish for not going with them. Still, I had me this feeling that they were headed into trouble. If I was right, then it wouldn't do for all three of us to be in the same boat.

After they'd disappeared from view I dismounted and hunkered down in the shade of a big spread-out oak whilst Old Dobbin, who I had groundhitched, nibbled on the sparse grass that grew under the trees. I kept a casual eye on him, knowing he'd hear anything or anyone long before I would. We'd been there maybe a half hour when I heard the two shots spaced close together, then silence.

Dang, I thought. My hunch was right.

I stood up, gathered up the reins, and stepped into the saddle. I headed back in the direction of the river and then swung north, figuring to come up on the back side of the camp, and then make my way in close to get the lay of the land.

Botrish had thought it was an Indian camp, but if it was, one thing was sure: they weren't friendly Indians. There was a good possibility, I thought, that they weren't Indians at all.

I hadn't gone very far when I stumbled across a faint trail running pretty much east and west, directly to where I figured the camp was. What disturbed me was the fresh hoofprints on that trail—made by shod horses. Poor a tracker as I am, I can at least tell a shod horse from a unshod one.

Ordinarily Indians didn't shoe their horses, which meant either the tracks were made by white men or the Indians had got hold of some white men's horses. I considered for about one a second before I gave up any idea of following the tracks. Instead, I kept on making my big circle around the camp.

It was late afternoon by the time I reached a spot opposite to where the Botrishes had left me. There was no more sound from the camp. I'd stopped from time to time to listen for someone following me, but there was nothing that I could hear or nothing that spooked the birds or other forest critters.

I tethered Old Dobbin to a tree and switched my boots for a pair of moccasins I carried in my saddlebags. With a piggin string, I tied my boots together and hung them around the saddle horn. Then I checked the hide-out knife strapped to my left leg. I settled down, with my back against a tree, to wait for dark. I wasn't about to go hunting for that camp in the daylight.

I was kind of dozing off when I heard a soft voice behind me say, "White man move, white man die."

"I ain't movin'," I said.

I looked over at Old Dobbin. He was grazing away, not paying much attention to anything except the grass he was chewing on. I had me two quick thoughts. One, that Old Dobbin was getting old, and two, that I was getting awful danged careless. This was twice today that someone had sneaked up on me whilst I dozed and this time Clara Botrish wasn't around to rescue me.

Moving without a sound, the Indian stepped around in front of me. He was a big man, almost as big as me, and real handsome. His face had no lines or wrinkles, but I noticed he was beginning to grey around the temples. Like almost all Indians he had no beard nor mustache. He was wearing buckskin pants and a buckskin shirt, and a Winchester rifle was slung over his shoulder. In his right hand he carried a U.S. Army bayonet; one edge of it I could see had been honed to razor sharpness.

I knew right off what would happen if I didn't do what he said, so I slouched back against the tree and looked up at him. "Where in the hell did you come from?" I demanded, still trying to gather my wits.

He answered with a question of his own. "Where did white man come from and what is he doing here on Indians' land?"

"Just passin' through," I said. "Not lookin' to bother no one or cause trouble."

He shook his head and looked at me skeptically. "All white men lie," he said.

"I reckon ya got a right to think that," I said. "Specially when yer carryin' that bayonet. What I'm tellin' ya is partly true though. I'm headin' for a town called Cutbank up north of here, lookin' for a feller named Frank Honerock."

A smile suddenly lit up the Indian's face.

"Me Chief Whitewater. Me Nez Perce Indian. Frank Honerock good friend. Friend of all Indians. You friend of Frank Honerock, Indian your friend."

"I got more to tell ya," I said, knowing one thing I *wouldn't* tell him was that I had never met Frank Honerock. If being Honerock's friend was going to keep me alive, then I was going to be his friend as long as that Indian was pointing his bayonet at me.

He listened real quiet whilst I told him about how I'd nearly been lynched by Bailey Harbor and how Zell Botrish and his daughter, Clara, had set me free and had come this far with me, and why I thought they might be in trouble.

He held up his left hand with the fingers spread wide apart. "Whitewater cross tracks of five white men riding on trail through forest. Maybe they find your friends."

"I thought there was a injun camp back in there," I said.

He shook his head. "No Indians here. Only me."

"What're you doin' here?" I asked.

He shrugged, but didn't answer.

"Look," I said. "Did you hear a couple of shots a while back?"

He nodded. "They come from direction where white men went."

I stared at him. "I think my friends are in trouble, if they ain't been kilt. Now that the sun's goin' down I got to go find out. You gonna let me go?"

He nodded and shoved the bayonet into a sheath that hung from his buckskins. "You go," he said. "Whitewater go with you. Frank Honerock, he would want that."

I reached my hand out and he took it and pulled me to my feet. "Let's go," I said.

He held out a big hand and stopped me. "Whitewater go first," he said, starting off into the woods.

CHAPTER 5

WHITEWATER MOVED at an easy pace, with me trailing close behind. We'd been walking maybe fifteen minutes when he stopped so suddenly I almost bumped into him.

"Smell smoke," he said.

"What now?" I asked.

"We go slow. We stay far apart," he said, starting off again.

I waited until he'd gone a little ways and then I followed after him, being careful not to step on any twigs or fallen branches that might crack underfoot. As we went, the smell of smoke grew stronger.

By now the sun was setting. The sky above was still light, but it was so dim down there amongst the trees it was hard for me to keep Whitewater in sight. I'd begun moving up closer so as not to lose him when he stopped again, and turned and beckoned to me. When I came up to him, I could see why he had stopped. Through the trees I caught the flicker of a campfire.

Now we moved slowly and carefully, from tree to tree, waiting each time to be sure we hadn't been seen or heard. Before long we reached a point where we had a clear view of the camp and could hear bits of what was being said.

The first man I saw was Bailey Harbor, the feller who old Pick Boone thought was headed for Helena. If he was, he hadn't got far before he changed his mind and circled back to get ahead of us. He was squatting by the fire holding a tin cup of coffee in both hands and looking at something beyond the fire and off to one side. Four other men were lazing around the fire. I looked where Harbor was looking and a chill went up my spine.

At first it looked like two more people were standing close together near a tree. A second look told me they were Zell and Clara Botrish and they were standing because they couldn't sit down. Their hands were tied behind their backs and around each of their necks was a noose. Both ropes was looped over a tree limb and pulled so tight both of the Botrishes were nearly standing on their tiptoes. Clara's shirt was ripped down the front and one breast was bare.

As Whitewater and me watched, Harbor got to his feet and strolled over to Botrish, still holding his cup of coffee.

"Like some coffee, Botrish?" he asked.

Botrish looked at him but didn't say anything.

"I said, ya want some coffee?" Harbor asked louder.

Botrish still stayed quiet.

"Well, here it is anyways, squaw man!" Harbor snarled and threw the hot coffee into Botrish's face. Botrish tried to duck and lost his balance, sagging against the rope. Even from where we were I could see he would strangle to death in a minute or two.

Before I could move, Harbor reached out and grabbed him by the front of his shirt and pulled him onto his feet.

"I ain't ready to hang ya yet," he snarled. "Soon, but not yet. I want ya to see what I do to yer breed daughter first."

He turned, stepped over close to Clara, reached out, and put a hand on her naked breast.

"Nice," he leered.

One of the men watching from around the fire called, "Save some for the rest of us, Bailey."

He laughed and reached for her again. "There's enough here for all of us, ain't there, honey?"

"We got to stop this," I whispered to Whitewater, but he was already bringing his rifle up.

"I'm going in," I said. "You cover me."

By now I had my six-gun in my hand. I stepped out of the trees and into the firelight.

"First one here who moves is a dead man," I said.

Suddenly it was so quiet you could have heard a pine needle drop.

Harbor turned and I could see him tense up, and his right hand dropped down near the butt of his gun.

"You want to live, Harbor, don't try it," I said. "On second thought, try it. It'll be fun killin' ya."

He relaxed. "Some other time," he said.

I motioned him with my gun. "Get over here with the others," I said.

As he started to move, a rifle shot rang out behind me and one of the men by the fire yelped in pain.

"I'm shot," he moaned, clutching his belly.

"Yer dead," I said. "And so is anyone else who tries somethin' funny. Come on in, Whitewater."

The big Indian stepped into the firelight, holding his rifle casual-like in his right hand and that sharpened bayonet in his left. He stepped over to where the Botrishes were standing and with two quick strokes of the bayonet he sliced through the ropes that formed the nooses.

Botrish started sliding to the ground, but Whitewater hooked one powerful arm around him and lowered him down easy onto the sod. Turning him on one side, he cut the ropes that bound his hands. Then he freed Clara, and she dropped down beside her father.

"He's been shot," she said.

"We'll look after him in a minute," I told her, keeping a careful eye on the men around the fire. "First we got to do something with these fellers here."

"Help me," the man Whitewater had shot moaned. "I'm gut shot. Oh, God. I'm dyin'. It hurts. Oh, God. It hurts."

Harbor looked at me. "Let me help him."

"He shouldn't of tried anythin'," I shrugged. "You fellers, one at a time, take yer guns and toss 'em over here. Ya try anythin' and if I don't shoot ya my friend over there will. Startin' with you, Harbor."

Careful, with his thumb and forefinger he lifted his pistol from its holster and tossed it at my feet. One by one the other three did the same.

"One of ya get his gun," I said, motioning at the wounded man who kept on moaning.

"All right," I said, when they'd tossed his gun on the pile. "All four of ya turn around and put yer hands behind yer backs. Clara, leave yer Pa a minute and bring some of that rope over here and tie these fellers good and tight."

Clara had managed to close the rip in her shirt with a hairpin, and she came over with the lengths of rope that Whitewater cut off her and her father, and one by one she tied their hands behind them. The last man she tied was Bailey Harbor.

When she was finished she said, "Mr. Harbor, please turn around."

He turned around slowly and looked at her with a kind of smirk. She stared back at him for a minute, then, without warning she hit him square in the mouth with her fist, putting all the weight of her body behind it.

Caught unawares, Harbor stumbled backward, tripped, and sat down hard in the middle of the fire, sending burning sticks and sparks flying in all directions. He gave a scream of terror and pain and rolled out of the fire onto the sod, squirming around and trying desperately to make certain his clothes weren't burning.

As he rolled around I could see his backside was all red and raw where the flames had burned through his jeans. He was lying on his side, moaning from pain and shame. Clara was wearing boots, and she walked over to him and kicked him hard in the stomach.

"Mr. Harbor," she said in a low, hate-filled voice, "if you ever lay a hand on me again I'll kill you."

He didn't say nothing, just laid there and moaned.

She turned to Whitewater. "Will you help me bring my father over by the fire?" she asked. "He's been shot and I need to take care of his wound."

The two of them went to help Botrish, and I went over to see how bad off the man Whitewater had shot was. He'd been quiet during the fuss with Harbor and it taken me just a glance to learn why. He was dead.

I walked around and and looked the other three in the face. They'd watched without a word while Clara beat up on Harbor. Two of them were with him the day he wanted to hang me. The third man I hadn't seen before.

"The feller Whitewater shot is dead," I informed them. "Any one of ya got anything for a burn?"

"I got some salve in my saddlebag," the third man said. "It's good for cuts and scrapes on a pony so it oughta be good fer burns on an ass."

I looked at the other two. "You two lie down on yer faces and don't move. Either of ya try somethin' and I'll come over and stomp ya. You"—to the third man—"I'm gonna untie ya and yer gonna get yer lineament or salve or whatever it is and yer gonna doctor ol' Bailey Harbor there."

In spite of myself I started to chuckle. "Dang," I said. "I don't know what's the funniest. Ol' Bailey Harbor rollin' around in the fire or the thought of him tryin' to sit in a saddle. He'll be needin' a pillow fer a while, at least."

The third man grinned. "He'll be ridin' shank's mare for the next week or two, all right."

Clara and Whitewater had helped Zell Botrish over by the fire and Clara had built it up again. Now she was bathing her father's left arm where a bullet had gone through it.

"He'll be all right," she said over her shoulder. "He just lost some blood is all."

The third man, who said his name was Guy Coe, led me to his saddlebag and I fished out the salve that he kept in an old snuff can.

"How about we put some on Botrish's wound?" I asked.

"Oughta help," he said.

So I took it to Clara, who smeared it on the wound in Botrish's arm where the bullet had gone in and also where it had come out.

"I guess ya better use the rest on yer pal," I said.

"He ain't no pal of mine," Coe said grimly. "I was just ridin' through town when one of these fellers asked me if I wanted to help chase down a cow thief. He must of meant you."

"He did," I said. "But I ain't no cow thief. He's a mean sonofabitch and I think he was lookin' for someone to hang just for fun."

I untied Coe's wrists and handed him the salve. "You fix him up and don't try nothin' funny."

"Mister?" he said questioningly.

"Tackett," I said.

"Sackett?" he said, surprise in his voice. "You ain't one of them there Sacketts?"

"Tackett," I said. "Not Sackett. Tackett."

"Man," he said, "yer big enough and mean enough to be one of them Sacketts."

"Go on and take care of Harbor, there," I said as we walked over to him. "Harbor, you turn over on yer belly, hear? Old Guy Coe is gonna doctor yer behind."

I turned back to Zell and Clara and motioned Chief Whitewater over. This here is Chief Whitewater," I said. "He's a Nez Perce. Used to run with Chief Joseph."

Botrish looked up from where he was sitting. "Howdy, Chief," he said. "Me and Clara owe ya. We won't ferget, will we, Clara?"

"We're grateful to you, Chief Whitewater," Clara said, then asked, "Aren't you a little far east for a Nez Perce?"

Whitewater nodded. "Chief Joseph surrender to the white man. Whitewater never surrender. Leave tribe first."

He looked boldly at Clara and gestured at Botrish. "You his squaw?"

She smiled. "I'm his daughter. My mother was a Sioux."

I broke in. "Botrish here and Clara was helpin' me get to Cutbank so's I could meet up with Frank Honerock when Harbor captured 'em."

I turned to Botrish. "You ain't told me what happened."

"Well," he said. "I was a damn fool. I figured Clara's people was camped here so we just rode on in. When we saw who it was it was too late. Harbor pulled his gun on me and when I went fer mine he shot me in the arm. After that they kicked us around a bit then tied us the way you seen us. They was tryin' to make me tell 'em where you was." He gave a lop-sided grin. "I would of, too, if I'd of knowed."

I looked at Botrish again and I could see now that he had really been kicked around. His left eye was bruised and nearly swollen shut, and his left lower lip was swollen, too, and caked with blood. Half of his face was red and beginning to blister where it was hit with the hot coffee Harbor had thrown at him.

Clara didn't look like she'd been bad hurt, but I noticed she was sucking on the knuckles of her right hand. She saw me looking and gave me a wicked grin.

"I cut it on Harbor's teeth when I hit him, but it was worth it. I just hope I don't get hydrophobia."

Just then Coe came up. "I've doctored old Bailey as best I could," he said, "but I didn't have nothin' for a bandage so I guess he's gonna have to go 'round the way he is 'til he gets back to the ranch. Oh, yeah, he asked me to untie him, but I figured I'd rather take my chances with you than with him. Thing is, if ya leave me with him now, he'll kill me sure. So I was wonderin', can I trail along with you all? And if I can't, will ya give me my pony and a head start?"

I turned to Botrish. "How 'bout it?"

"Let him come along," Botrish said. "He tried to stop 'em but there wasn't much he could do if he wanted to save his own hide."

"All right," I said to Coe. "You can come along but don't try playin' no games. The chief here can take yer head off with that bayonet he carries, can't ya, Chief?"

Whitewater nodded and smiled the ghost of a smile. "Use it to take scalps, too." he said.

He turned to Clara and said something in Indian talk and she, sounding kind of surprised, answered him and then turned to me.

"He speaks Sioux," she said, "as well as the Nez Perce dialect and English."

"Who's this Chief Joseph feller?" I asked, curious.

"He's a famous Indian warrior," she said. "The chief of the Nez Perce. He fought the white man a long time but finally had to surrender. Chief Whitewater was an important man in the tribe, too. My people know of him. He chose to leave the tribe rather than surrender."

Whilst we were talking, I had built up the fire again, pushing back into it the burning sticks that Harbor scattered with his thrashing around. I fished around in Harbor's supplies and before long I'd fried up some bacon, heated some beans, and made a fresh pot of coffee.

"I'm headin' for Cutbank in the morning," I said to Botrish between sips of coffee. "What're you aimin' to do?"

"Me and Clara still wanta tag along," he replied. "We didn't leave nothin' in Kolakoka we can't afford to lose. We go back there and ol' Tod Websterby 'll give us a bad time for sure. 'Sides, I been in Cutbank afore. Fact is, it's not a bad place and Frank Honerock, from what I hear, he's a good man."

Just then Chief Whitewater said, "Riders come." He picked up his rifle and bayonet and faded into the darkness. The Botrishes, Coe, and me did likewise, leaving our prisoners in the ring of firelight.

In a minute I heard the sound of hoofs and then a voice called, "Holloa, the camp! Can we come in?"

"Come in careful-like," I called back.

There were two of them. One, Sheriff Curt von Cart, I knew. The other—a slender, grey-haired man, dressed more like a townsman than a rancher—was a stranger.

They dismounted stiffly. "Been a long day," von Cart said, as I stepped out of the dark. "This here is Evan Peryea. We been hopin' to catch up with you."

"Peryea?" I said. "Oh, yeah. Yer the feller with the soda water springs."

"It's better than that," he said. "It's good stuff. Delicious and refreshing, both."

"I ever go back to Kolakoka, I'll stop by and try some," I said.

The sheriff interrupted us. He had spotted our prisoners. "Who you got here?" he said.

"Friends of yourn," I said. "Ol' Bailey Harbor and two of his boys."

He gave a low whistle. "You sure been busy today, Tackett, you'n my deputy there."

Botrish had joined us as von Cart talked.

"Yep," he went on. "You been busy, all right. We come across Willie Brown, the kid from the livery stable, and untied him and sent him home. I hope he's smart enough to stay there. Then we come across two of Websterby's men hoofin' it toward town. Said someone had stole their horses. Now danged if you ain't got old Bailey Harbor and two of his men all hogtied. Mind tellin' me what's goin' on?"

Before I could answer Harbor snarled, "Don't just stand there, von Cart. Untie us and arrest these men."

"I wouldn't if I was you, Sheriff," I said.

"Websterby'll have yer neck if ya don't," Harbor shouted.

I went over and looked down at him. "You keep talkin'," I said, "and I'm gonna stomp yer face."

He glared at me but clamped his lips tight shut, not wanting to see if I was serious.

"Lemme start from the beginnin', Sheriff," I said.

CHAPTER 6

WHEN I FINISHED telling von Cart what had gone on he just shook his head.

"Ya know," he said, "there's some fellers, wherever they go trouble follers 'em. Yer one of them fellers. I don't know why ya had to come through here. Everything was quiet afore ya got here."

"Sheriff," I said, "I sure didn't come here lookin' fer trouble. I was just passin' through and old Bailey Harbor there got it in his head to hang me. Shucks! *You* know that. You stopped him and I'm almighty grateful. Like I told ya before, all I'm tryin' to do is get up to Cutbank and see if Frank Honerock can point me to a feller named Tackett. He may be kinfolk.

"Fact is, Sheriff, I'm headin' for Cutbank in the mornin'. Don't never expect to come this way again, not even for a taste of Mr. Peryea's bubbly spring water."

"'Fraid it ain't that simple, son," von Cart said. "Ya may of forgot, but yer an escaped prisoner so I'm gonna have to take ya back. And Zell here, when ya think about it, I got to arrest him for aidin' and abettin'. I'll see you both get a fair trial, though. Right now yer under arrest."

"Dang it, Sheriff," I said. "I was hopin' we could work this out peaceful-like 'cause I'm a peaceful man by nature. But I ain't going back with ya. Zell here, now he can do what he pleases, but like I said, me I'm heading for Cutbank in the mornin'."

"And Clara and me'll be trailin' along with ya," Botrish said, speaking from the shadows he'd slipped into. "And, Von, you ain't arrestin' no one. Right now there's three guns on you and Peryea, and that don't count Tackett's. So right now why don't you and Evan drop yer guns. That way nobody'll get hurt."

"Now look here—," von Cart started out.

"Drop 'em, I said," Botrish interrupted. "I ain't gonna tell ya again."

After dropping his gun slowly and carefully, von Cart turned so he was facing Botrish.

"Zell," he said, "you can run but ya can't hide. You and Tackett both. Even if I wasn't to come after ya with a posse, Websterby and Harbor'll run the two of ya down if they have to chase ya to hell and back."

"We'll risk it, Sheriff," I said. "Besides, old Bailey Harbor there ain't about to chase anyone for a while, 'less'n he does it on foot. Clara, you go ahead and tie these fellers up, too, and Coe, you come on in and take care of their horses. Zell, you been beat up pretty bad so you get some rest. Clara and Coe and me'll take turns standin' guard."

About then it occurred to me that it had been a while since we'd seen Chief Whitewater.

"Where's the chief?" I asked. Nobody knew.

"Chief!" I called. There was no answer.

"Looks like he taken off," I said.

"Injuns are notional," Coe said.

Funny, I thought. That's what Clara says about white men.

I turned back to von Cart and Peryea, who Clara was busy tying up.

"I finally figured how I'm gonna work this, Sheriff," I said, squatting down beside him. "In the mornin', I'm gonna take Peryea with us a ways, then I'm gonna turn him loose on foot. He can come back and turn the rest of you loose if he feels like it. Oh yeah, I'm gonna turn yer horses loose tonight. Maybe they won't wander too far. Hard to tell. Anyways, if they do they'll prob'ly head fer home.

"I'll keep yer guns, too. I'll leave 'em with Frank Honerock up at Cutbank. You can pick 'em up there."

Von Cart gave me a friendly smile. "See here, son, ya wouldn't do that. Ya can't leave us unarmed and afoot. Ya can't tell who we might run into. Injuns or outlaws or even a grizzly bear."

"Best advice I can give ya, Sheriff," I said, "is walk careful."

Von Cart quit smiling. "I shoulda let Harbor hang ya that first time," he growled. "I won't make that mistake again."

"Sleep good," I grinned and walked over to the fire and poured me a mug of coffee. It was hot and black and tasted good. Clara joined me by the fire.

"What about them?" she asked, gesturing at our prisoners. "Shall I feed them?"

"Let 'em eat cake," I said.

She looked at me quizzically. "How do you know that saying?"

"Read it somewheres," I said casually.

"A lot of cowboys can't read," she said. "You're one of the lucky ones."

I nodded agreement, not telling her that I only learned in the last year and I still didn't read very good. But I was getting better, and one reason was, now that I knew how, I read whenever I could, whatever I could find—newspapers, books, even the labels on cans and bottles.

Esmeralda had brought a lot of books with her from the East and insisted that I read them any time I had the chance. So I read some of the great English writers like ol' Charles Dickens and that woman Jane Austen. Plus I also read Americans like Edgar Allan Poe, Mark Twain, James Fenimore Cooper, Bret Harte, and some others.

Fact was, I had two of Esme's books packed in my saddlebags, but ever since I'd run into Bailey Harbor I hadn't had much chance to read them or anything else. One was *Grimm's Fairy Tales,* stories some German fellers wrote fer young'uns, and the other was Twain's *Innocents Abroad.*

I'd always had the idea that folks who wrote real honest-to-goodness literature were long dead, but Esme told me that Harte and Stevenson and Twain were still alive.

"I've met Mr. Clemens," she said, explaining to me that Twain's real name was Samuel Clemens. She also told me that Twain and Stevenson and Harte had all lived and worked in the West.

Well, anyways, I shook off those book thoughts and told Clara to get some sleep. When she'd turned in I went to Coe and told him it would just be him and me standing guard and for him to wake me up when it was my turn. Then I took my bedroll and spread it at the edge of the clearing, in the shadows away from the fire. I wasn't aiming to be a sitting duck for nobody.

Tired as I was I couldn't sleep, I was that uneasy. I laid my six-gun in easy reach and put my boots back on in case of trouble. I wasn't expecting any but I was going to be ready just in case.

Several things were nagging at me. In the first place I'm a law-respecting man and I didn't like holding Sheriff von Cart prisoner even if he had ducked out back in Kolakoka and left me at the mercy of Tod Websterby's lynch mob. Besides, I knew if he followed me to Cutbank he could cause me trouble with the sheriff there. And what he'd said about Websterby and Harbor was prob'ly true. Once Harbor's burns had healed he and Websterby would follow me to Cutbank or hell itself. Harbor would be wanting to get even and Websterby would stand by his foreman. One day, I knew, I would have to face them. I wished then I had tough Jack Sears with me, but he was dead now, or Blackie Harrington and Lew Haight, two solid hands from the R-Bar-R who'd stood with me in more than one tight spot.

Guy Coe had thought I was one of the Sacketts and this was one of those times I wished I was. They were a family of gunfighters from the hills of Tennessee who had settled in southern Colorado and along the northern New Mexico border, and when you took on one of them you took on all of them. Me, I was just a big old mountain boy from the Sierra Nevada gold camps, with no kinfolk that I knew of now that Ma was dead.

I thought again about the Tackett who had a place up somewhere near Cutbank. What if he was my Pa? That was something I had to find out, even though I knew the chances of my father being alive were not much better than zero. And if the Tackett up there in the Cutbank country wasn't Pa, who was he? Was he kin, or just some-body who shared my last name? I needed to know that, too. And no sheriff nor lynch mob was going to stop me. Thinking that way, I was drifting off to sleep when I heard a soft voice whispering, "Tackett."

I didn't move.

The voice came again, "Tackett."

I sat up. "Where ya been, Chief?" I asked.

Moving silently Chief Whitewater squatted down beside me.

"Seven white men camp a little ways from here," he said in a low voice.

"Websterby? I asked.

"Me not know Websterby," he said. "Boss man has white hair, white beard. That Websterby?"

"Danged if I know," I said. "Wait here. I'll find out."

I went to where Botrish was lying. He was sleeping restless and he woke as soon as I touched him. "Websterby," I said. "White hair? White beard?"

"Yeah," he said. "Why?"

"He's camped nearby. I'm thinkin' we better be thinkin' about movin' out."

Botrish didn't say anything. He just rolled out of his blankets and began awkwardly rolling them with his good hand. I left him and went to Coe who was sitting near the fire.

"We're moving out now," I said. "Don't say nothin'. I'll explain later."

Then I woke Clara. She nodded her understanding and began breaking camp. I went and woke up Peryea, untied him, and warned him not to try anything but to come along peaceful.

In ten minutes we had the horses saddled and were ready to go. Coe turned our prisoners' horses loose, gave each one a swat on the flank, and our little group set off, headed north toward Cutbank. Somewhere Chief Whitewater had picked up a horse for hisself, and he led the way. Clara and Botrish followed and me and Coe brought up the rear.

We were soon out of the forest, riding north up a narrow valley between two ranges of mountains. It was a dark night with just the sliver of a moon, but Whitewater moved steady and unhesitating along the faint trail. After about an hour he turned off suddenly into the mountains on our east. I stopped there for just a minute and told Peryea to dismount.

"Take off," I said, "and don't even think about teamin' up with Websterby and them. Not if ya wanta live to drink yer bubbly water."

He didn't say anything but headed on back down the trail.

After he'd gone Whitewater, led us through a defile barely wide enough in some places for a man on horseback to ride through without scraping his stirrups on both sides. In other places it was more than wide enough for the five of us to ride abreast.

The defile twisted and turned but kept heading in a generally easterly direction. It climbed, sometimes gently and sometimes steep, for another hour then began descending sharply 'til finally it widened out and we rode onto an alluvial fan on the east side of the mountains.

"Hold up, Chief," I called, reining in Old Dobbin.

Whitewater pulled up his horse, one of those appaloosas that the Nez Perce seemed to take to, and came back to me.

"We need to stop for a while, Chief," I said. "Botrish don't look like he can go much farther without restin' and gettin' some food into him. One of us can go back up the canyon a ways and listen to see if someone's comin'. A lone man could hold off an army back there."

Whitewater nodded. "Camping place near here. You come."

He led off again, heading north on a narrow trail that led along the slope of the mountain. We'd gone less than a hundred yards when he stopped. There at the base of a large rock I made out a small pool with a tiny trickle of water flowing from it and losing itself in the soft soil of the fan. Off to one side there were signs of a lot of campfires. Problem was, there wasn't any wood for a new fire. But there was brush and debris and deadwood scattered about back in the canyon, so whilst the others were making camp I went back there to hunt for firewood.

At the head of the canyon I tied Old Dobbin to a bush, traded my boots for the moccasins again, and went looking. I walked up the canyon a ways figuring to pick up sticks and twigs on my way back to Old Dobbin.

I'd gone maybe fifty yards when I heard a familiar noise. It was the sound of a horseshoe striking a stone. I slid back into the darker shadows along the wall of the canyon. Snaking my gun from its holster, I stood there hardly breathing. The click sounded again, this time nearer. Straining my eyes in the dark, I finally saw a darker blob that had to be a horse and rider moving down the canyon toward me.

"Pull up, Mister, or yer a dead man," I said as he came even with where I stood.

But he didn't. Instead, he dug his spurs in, let out a whoop, and taken off down the canyon. His action caught me by surprise, and besides I hadn't no intention of shooting at him. A shot echoing through that narrow canyon would have made enough noise to waken the dead, and a stray bullet like as not could nick Old Dobbin who wasn't that far off.

I hurried down the canyon after the strange rider, but when I reached the spot where I had tethered Old Dobbin he wasn't there. The rider's whoop and the sounds of the galloping horse must of startled him so he pulled loose from the bush I had tied him to. I knew he hadn't gone far, but in the dark I couldn't see which way he'd gone.

Cursing under my breath, I picked up a few sticks of wood and headed back to where the others were camped. When I got to the pool of water, Coe spoke up from the darkness by the rock: "That you, Tackett?"

"It's me," I said.

"What was that commotion?" he asked. "Where's yer horse?"

"There's a rider out there somewheres and he scared Old Dobbin off. I'll find him when it gets light. Right now I'm worried about that rider. Who in tarnation is he and why's he followin' us—if he is?"

We came up to the others and I told them what had happened. "Best we make a cold camp. Don't want to give that feller anything to shoot at if he means us no good."

Zell Botrish was lying on his bedroll, not saying nothing. "You all right?" I asked.

"I'll make it," he grunted. "But I could sure use some coffee."
Whitewater touched me on the arm. "You come."

I followed him around to the back side of the rock. Other rocks
had tumbled down around it, blocking the view from both sides.

"Build fire here," he said. "We watch in front."

I fetched the wood I'd brought from the canyon and built a tiny
fire up against the rock. Clara joined me, bringing a coffee pot full
of water and a handful of the coffee she'd found in the saddlebags
of one of Harbor's men. In a few minutes she had made enough
coffee for all of us except Chief Whitewater who refused a mugful.

"Indian only drink water," he said.

We sat there in the dark nursing our coffee. Clara came over and
sat beside me. "Father says he's feeling better," she said. "But I don't
believe him. I felt him and he's running a fever. I'm afraid he's got
an infection."

"Coe knows this part of the country and he tells me we're gettin'
close to Cutbank, I said. "We'll leave here at daylight and if we push
it we ought to get to Cutbank before dark. There'll be somebody
there who can help, maybe even a doctor."

"I keep hoping we'll run across my people," she said. "But I think
now we may be on the wrong side of the mountain. They usually
camp on the evening side of the hill."

CHAPTER 7

OLD DOBBIN MUST of been attracted by the smell of the smoke or the coffee because he came wandering in trailing his reins just as I was unrolling my bedroll. I taken a few minutes to rub him down and picketed him nearby. The rest of the night I slept with one eye open, but it passed peaceful enough with only the occasional bark of a coyote or the call of a nightbird to break the stillness. Now I'm not much of a tracker, but I know the sounds of the wilderness and I can tell the hoot of a owl from the hoot of a human trying to sound like a owl. If there was any humans out there that night, they kept mighty quiet.

Clara had volunteered to keep watch during the hours before dawn so she could keep a cold cloth on her father's forehead, so Coe and me grabbed some shuteye. Whitewater had disappeared into the night again. I hoped he might show up in the morning, but I had no way of knowing. He was a strange one, that Indian, showing up out of nowhere the way he had, and then staying around to lend a hand when it was desperately needed. I couldn't quite figure him out. He said he'd fallen out with Chief Joseph after the chief made peace with the white man, but here he was helping us— and not just because Clara was half Indian, either. I shrugged. I was glad enough for his help. I'd worry about the why of it later.

I rolled out just as the stars were beginning to dim. Clara had already stirred up the fire and added a few sticks she'd gathered somewhere, and I could smell coffee boiling and bacon frying. First thing I did was go looking for a patch of grass where Old Dobbin might graze a bit, but there wasn't none. So I taken him and the other horses to water at the spot where the stream trickled out of the pool and lost itself in the alluvial sand. By the time I finished that chore, Coe joined me and the two of us saddled our own horses and the Botrishes'.

Back at the fire Clara and her father were waiting for us. Zell Botrish looked a mess, with half of his face blistered by the hot coffee Harbor had thrown at him and his lips swollen and cut from the beating Harbor and his men had given him earlier. But there was a sparkle in his eyes and he was moving easier. Clara had worked up a sling for his wounded arm, and otherwise he seemed fine.

"I'm fine," he said when I asked how he was feeling. "Fever seems to be all gone out of my arm. That lineament Coe uses is good stuff."

Clara looked surprisingly good. She'd brushed her long black hair until it shone, and during the night she'd fetched a needle and thread from her pack and sewed up her torn shirt. She noticed me looking and turned away, embarrassed-like.

"We'll find ya a new dress in Cutbank," I said.

"You're kind," she said. "But I have another one in my pack. I wanted to save it until we got to town."

Just then Old Dobbin threw up his head and whinnied.

"Someone comin'," I said and we all faded into the rocks.

A minute later two riders came in sight. One was Chief Whitewater and the other, looking to be Whitewater's prisoner, was our young friend Willie, the stable hand.

I stepped out from behind the rock. "What ya got there, Chief?"

Whitewater almost smiled. "Find papoose sleeping near main trail. Bring him here to see what you want done with him."

"Howdy, Willie," I said. "When ya gonna learn not to bother grown-ups?"

"Go to hell," Willie snarled, twisting his hairless upper lip into what he must have thought was a tough sneer.

"Did he have a gun, Chief?" I asked.

Whitewater reached into his belt and pulled out a Colt .45 six-shooter.

"Gimme it back and I'll take on one or both of ya," Willie bragged.

I strolled over to where Willie was sitting in his saddle and yanked him to the ground. Holding him by the front of his shirt, I lifted him up 'til he was eye to eye with me.

"Son," I said, ignoring his struggles, "yer gonna get yerself kilt if ya don't start gettin' some horse sense."

I lowered him to the ground again but kept hold of his shirt front, and danged if he didn't try to knee me. I turned sideways and caught his knee on my left thigh. I started to backhand him but changed my mind at the last second, and shoved him away from me.

He stumbled back and stood there glaring at me.

"Son," I said, "ya wanta fight me?"

"I ain't fool enough to take ya on with my fists, but make that injun gimme back my gun and I'll fight ya. If ya ain't yella, that is."

"I don't wanta kill ya, Willie," I said.

"Yer yella," he said loudly.

I sighed. "Toss him his gun, Chief."

Whitewater shrugged and tossed Willie his gun. Willie caught it in his right hand, whirled and shot. I yanked my own six-shooter out of the holster and leveled it at him, but didn't shoot. Instead I watched his jaw drop as the hammer of his gun clicked on empty and clicked again.

"Gun's empty, Willie," I drawled. "The chief unloaded it whilst you was shootin' off yer face."

White-faced and shaky, Willie dropped his gun into its holster. "Ya could of kilt me," he mumbled. "Ya could of kilt me."

"I could of," I agreed. "But I didn't have no intention of it. Killin' a man is a serious matter, Willie. So is just drawin' a gun on another man. Ya kill a man and you've took a human life and ya can't never get it back and ya ought to think long and careful about that. Ya draw a gun on another man and instead of you killin' him he might kill you, like I could of kilt ya a minute ago.

"Killin' another man don't make a hero out of ya, Willie. Don't even make ya a big man. But ya draw just a mite slower than the other feller and that fer sure makes you a dead man. That's somethin' else ya ought to think about, Willie.

"Now, how about some coffee?"

I went over and put an arm around his shoulders and walked him over to the campfire. He was still white-faced and I could feel him shaking. Botrish and Coe and Clara, who'd watched the goings on, were sitting by the fire drinking coffee. None of them said a word.

Clara found a tin cup in her pack and poured coffee for Willie who took it, mumbled a "thankya, ma'am," and squatted silently on his haunches, sipping on it.

Whitewater had joined us but after standing by the fire a while he said, "I go now. I see you again, maybe."

He stood and in white man's fashion gravely shook hands with each of us, including Willie. Then he turned to his horse, mounted, and rode slowly down the side of the mountain, heading due east into the sunrise. He never looked back.

"There goes a real man," I said. "We'd of been in deep trouble without he hadn't come along."

"If," Clara said.

"What?" I asked.

"Nothing," she said. "You're right. We would have been in deep trouble without he hadn't come along."

"Yer funnin' me," I said.

"Teasing," she said.

I looked at her blankly.

"I'm sorry," she said. "I didn't mean to. We'd have been in deep trouble, Dad and I, if *you* hadn't come along."

She reached out and gently touched my unshaven cheek.

Dang, I didn't need that. There was a special girl back at the R-Bar-R and we'd be married as soon as I got back. Last thing I needed was another girl going soft on me. Or me on her, for that matter.

I turned to Zell. "How far do you reckon it is to Cutbank?"

"A hard day's ride yet, I reckon," he said. "Oughta come on to it day after tomorrow, easy."

"I reckon we'd best get goin'," I said. "Willie, I'm gonna let you go only don't let me catch you comin' after us again. You do, I'm likely to ferget yer wet behind the ears."

Willie looked at me like he was about to bust out crying.

"Mr. Tackett," he said in a voice that shook just a little. "I'd admire to trail along with ya. I can carry my weight and ya might need a extra hand somewheres along the line."

I looked around at the Botrishes and at Coe.

"Up to you," Zell said, finally.

"Come on then, Willie," I said. "And, by the way, was that you come through the canyon last night?"

"Uh huh," he said. "I'd been follerin' ya, but I almost missed ya when ya turned into that canyon. When ya told me to stop I thought I was a gonner, sure. Good thing ya didn't shoot or I might of been. That's twice ya could of kilt me."

"Let's head out," I said.

I led our little party off the alluvial fan and then headed just a little bit east of due north in the general direction of where Zell Botrish figured Cutbank should be. It was rolling grass country cut through on occasion by a dry wash or a small creek. At noon we topped a small rise and rode down to the banks of a tree-lined creek.

"We'll stop here and rest a while. Let the horses graze a mite," I said.

Two hundred yards away a lone buffalo was feeding, paying no mind to the humans and horses resting nearby.

"Chance to get some fresh meat," Coe said, nodding at the buffalo.

"Go ahead," I said.

"I'll go with him," Willie volunteered.

"We'll do it slow and easy," Coe told him, and they began walking their horses toward the buffalo. They hadn't gone but a few yards when the buffalo took three steps, staggered, and fell over, and at the same time the sound of a rifle shot echoed past us. A second later two Indians appeared from the line of trees along the creek just opposite the buffalo. We'd been hidden from them, first by the hill and then by that line of trees.

I heard Willie holler "Damn them," saw him yank his six-gun from its holster and at the same time jab his horse in the flanks with his spurs. The horse leaped forward and Coe, who was a little ahead of

Willie, reacted with a speed I hadn't thought he had. As Willie's horse raced by, Coe left his saddle in a flying leap. He missed Willie's body, but he caught hold of the boy's thigh. Willie's horse ran on but Coe and Willie, with Coe hanging on tight to Willie's leg, tumbled to the ground and laid there for a minute, stunned.

Then Coe slowly got to his feet. Looking down at Willie, he began to curse him with every cuss word I ever knew and some I'd never heard before. Willie just laid there white-faced, looking up at him.

I dismounted and walked over to where he was laying. I reached down, grabbed a hand, and yanked him to his feet. He looked ready to cry from hurt and shame.

"That was a damn fool trick, Son," I said. "Ya don't know how many injuns there are around here. Ya don't know if they're friendly or not. Ya could of brang a whole tribe down around our heads."

"They done stole our buffalo," Willie said, taking a deep breath.

"Maybe we was about to steal theirs," I said. "This is their land, has been for a thousand years or more. You and me, we're trespassin.' At least in their minds."

In back of me Zell Botrish said, "Tackett. Take a look."

I looked over to where we'd first seen the Indians. There were ten of them now and they were riding toward us. I noticed with relief that they were not wearing war paint.

"Dad," I heard Clara say "that looks like Eagle Beak."

"Sure enough," Botrish said. "Tackett, that there is Clara's cousin. These are the folks we was lookin' for yesterday. They're farther east of the Sun than I expected. Let me do the talkin'."

The Indians drew up and stopped about fifteen feet from us.

"Howdy, Eagle Beak," Botrish said, holding his hand up, palm out, in the traditional gesture of friendship.

"How," Eagle Beak said, also holding his hand up. "You bring Dancing Deer back to her people."

"Dancing Deer," I said. "Yer Dancing Deer?"

"That's my Indian name," Clara said. "I've always liked it. It's a pretty name, don't you think?"

Botrish shook his head at Eagle Beak. "Clara's stayin' with us. We got some bad white men chasin' us. We're hopin' to get to Cutbank afore they catch up to us."

"Cutbank day's ride away," Eagle Beak said. "You stay and eat. You leave Dancing Deer here."

"We'll stay and eat," Botrish agreed. "Then we'll be movin' along. Clara, too."

Botrish gestured at Coe and Willie and me. "These here are our friends. We ride together. Them there are Willie and Coe and this big galoot is Tackett."

Eagle Beak's narrow eyes widened. "You Sackett. Sacketts come to Sioux country before, maybe ten summers ago. They hunt with Sioux. They friends of Sioux. You friend of Sioux?"

"I'm a friend of the Sioux," I answered. "But I'm Tackett, not Sackett. There are many Sacketts. But there's only one Tackett— me."

"You Sackett," Eagle Beak insisted. "You friend. You welcome to stay with Sioux."

"Thanks," I said. "We'll eat and then we'll be driftin'."

We followed the Indians back to their camp which was nearly a mile away and on the north side of the creek. Clara, or Dancing Deer, rode alongside Eagle Beak and they talked all the way to camp. Four of the Indians dropped off to skin the buffalo and bring the meat and the hide to the camp.

There were about forty people at the camp. The men was all ages, from boys still in their teens to an old man about fifty, the chief of this small band of Teton Sioux.

He'd once been a tall and handsome brave, but now his face was lined and he walked with a limp—the reminder of a white soldier's bullet, Eagle Beak explained.

His name was Spotted Owl and he was Eagle Beak's father and Clara's uncle. Speaking Sioux, with Clara translating for us, he welcomed us to camp. But as he went on talking I noticed Clara and her father getting more and more edgy. When Spotted Owl finished talking, I asked Clara if there was a problem.

"Spotted Owl is insisting that I stay," she said. "He says I belong with the tribe and not with the white man. He says either I stay or the rest of you can't leave."

"Dang," I said. "That's mighty unfriendly of him. What do ya think we ought to do?"

Willie, who'd been listening, butted in, "I say we shoot our way out. They ain't much."

"Back off, kid," Coe said. "Yer too eager to get someone kilt."

"It's all right," Clara said. "I've taken care of it. He says we can go after we eat."

"What'd ya tell him?" I asked.

She gave a small laugh. "I told him we were going to Cutbank because you and I were going to get married there."

"Dang it. Ya shouldn't of—"

"It was all I could think of," she said.

"Well, I reckon it's all right.He won't never know whether or not we got married."

"He wants to come along and bring Eagle Beak," she told me. "He says he's never seen a white man's wedding before. Besides, he says, the Sioux are friends of the Sacketts and they wish to honor you with their presence at your wedding."

"Look, Clara," I said. "First off, as ya dang well know, I ain't no Sackett. Sometimes I wisht I was but I ain't. And in the second place I can't marry ya and ya dang well know that, too. There's a girl waitin' fer me back down in Arizona."

"I remember," she said, giggling. "You'll just have to figure something out before we get to Cutbank."

CHAPTER 8

"COE," I SAID. "I got a problem and I need yer help. Yers and Willie's"

Whilst Clara and Zell talked up old times with her Indian kinfolk I had drawn the other two to one side. I quick told them what Clara had told me.

"I still think we oughta take 'em on," Willie said, patting the gun at his side.

Coe gave him a disgusted look. "What d'ya got on yer mind?" he asked me.

"I been thinkin'," I said. "If I was to take off runnin' they'd prob'ly let me go. Same thing if you two come with me. But then they'd make Clara stay. That's dead sure. Her and Zell, both. And I can't let that happen to 'em. Clara deserves better than spendin' the rest of life in a tepee with some injun brave.

"Then, too, there's always the chance they'd foller us, injuns bein' notional and all. And I ain't interested in bein' their guest if they decide they got a grudge against us."

"Let 'em try somethin'," Willie said toughlike, patting his gun again.

"Fer the last time, kid, shut up," Coe growled.

Willie glared at him a second, then looked away. Coe was a tough man and Willie knew it. Maybe, I thought, he's beginning to smarten up.

I went on: "So what I wanta do is this. I want Clara to tell 'em I got to get into town in a hurry to find us a preacher and a place to get hitched. I'll take Willie with me. It's better that way fer a lot of reasons. But mainly I need a good hand with me."

Willie gave me a looked of pride mixed with dog-like devotion and I patted him on the shoulder.

"That means you gotta stay here with Clara and Zell overnight and come along in the morning, you and them and them two injuns who wanta come to the weddin'."

"Ya think they'll go fer that?" Coe asked.

"It'll be up to Clara to convince 'em," I replied as we walked over to where Clara and Zell were still jawing with Spotted Owl and Eagle Beak.

I beckoned Clara over to me, put my arm around her like maybe I was the man she was going to marry, and walked her over to where I could talk to her in private. "Here's my plan," I said. As I outlined it, a look of disappointment crossed her face for just a second, but then she smiled.

"I think it will work as long as Guy Coe stays here as insurance," she said. "If it was just father and me I think they'd keep us here and make us go with them to their next camping ground."

"Ya got to play yer part," I said. "Since it was yer idea that we're gettin' married ya gotta, well, you know, ya gotta—"

"I gotta kiss you good-bye," she said, giggling again. "And I will. Believe me, I will."

I felt myself turning red under my whiskers. "Ya don't have to overdo it."

"They're watching us right now," she said looking around me to where the others were waiting.

Standing on her tiptoes she reached up, pulled my head down, and kissed me fiercely on the lips.

Dang it, Del, I thought. You better be careful. There's a special girl waitin' fer you in Arizona.

But I had to admit she tasted good.

Stepping back, Clara looked me square in the eyes. "That's just a sample," she said. Then, taking my hand, she led me back to the others.

In a minute she was back to jabbering at them in Sioux. When she finished talking, Spotted Owl nodded and turned to me.

"You go, Tackett," he said. "Tomorrow we come. Bring Dancing Deer. She will be your squaw by the white man's law. Then we return here for Indian wedding. Until then you sleep in separate tepees."

"Indian way good way," I said.

Turning to Willie I said, "Let's saddle up, pardner. We've a hard ride ahead."

Coe joined us as we cinched our saddles up. "Ya fergot to tell me. What happens when we get to Cutbank?"

"Danged if I know," I said, putting a foot in the stirrup and swinging into the saddle. "Maybe I'll marry her."

We taken off at a fast trot, heading in the general direction of Cutbank. I was riding Old Dobbin and Willie rode a scrawny pinto that looked trail-worn but acted full of beans. After about an hour we came to a trail that I took to be the road to Cutbank. It was wide enough for two of us to ride abreast, wide enough even for a stagecoach, although I didn't see any fresh wheel tracks. We got off and walked the horses to give them a breather and I had my first real chance to talk to Willie.

"Yer folks'll be missin' you," I said.

"Ain't got none."

That kind of took me aback. I knew what it was to be alone in the world.

"What happened?" I asked.

"Rustlers kilt my old man when I was a little kid. Then Ma moved us into town 'cause there wasn't nothin' for us on the ranch. Ma couldn't afford no help and the rustlers got all our cows. Ma complained to the sheriff and he looked around a mite but didn't arrest no one. When we moved to town, Ma, she worked at the general store 'til she took sick a while back and died. I been on my own since."

"How old are ya, Willie?"

"Be sixteen next month."

I chuckled. "That's about the right age to be out on yer own. When I was sixteen my Ma sent me off. Said it was time I made my own way."

"What happened to yer Ma?"

"She died a while back. I never seen her again 'cause I never went home again. Allus meant to but never got around to it."

"But ya could of gone home?"

"Yep."

"Well, I can't," he said, his voice shaking.

I reached over and squeezed his shoulder. "Nobody really can, Willie. Ya go away for a while and when ya go back you find things have changed and folks have changed and what's between folks, that's changed, too. Things just ain't the same. That's why if ya love someone, ya shouldn't really never leave 'em."

"Heard ya talkin' about havin' a sweetheart in Arizona. You went off and left her."

"Yeah, I know," I said. "And it was prob'ly a mistake. "I'm prob'ly a damn fool. I went off and left the sweetest, purtiest girl in the world. And the sweetest dog, too."

"I never had no dog," he said wistfully.

"Beauty's a big, black dog," I said. "Saved my life once."

We rode quiet-like for a ways, then he asked, "How come ya went and left 'em?"

"It's kind of a long story," I said. "It has to do with my Pa. I never knowed him. He went off to fight in the War Between the States and never come back. As far as I know, him and Ma was the only kin I had. Shucks, boy, I never even heard of anyone else named Tackett 'til just a few weeks ago. Then the word come down from a feller up in Cutbank that there was a man named Tackett ranchin' up this way. I just couldn't sit by and not find out if he's kinfolk, so I headed north. Soon as I know for sure, I'm goin' back to Arizona."

"I got kinfolk down in Missouri," Willie said. "I been thinkin' of headin' that way."

I didn't answer. I was too busy asking myself some questions. What was I doing up in this part of the country anyway? And when I came right down to it, what did it matter if there was a Tackett up here or not? I'd gone near thirty years without knowing him or anyone else named Tackett. What really mattered was the girl I loved was in Arizona. And that's where I belonged.

I reined in Old Dobbin sharply. Why not head home now?
Willie pulled up, too. "Somethin' wrong?"

I shook my head and kicked Old Dobbin lightly in the flanks.
"Nothin'." I said. "Let's go."

Just before dark we forded a small stream, then rode upstream a
little ways from the trail to make camp.

"There's cows on this side of the stream," Willie said. "First I've seen."

"Means we're gettin' close," I said. "Prob'ly get there by noon
tomorrow."

We unsaddled the horses and rubbed them down with dry grass,
then picketed them where they could graze out of sight from the
trail. I made coffee and warmed some beans over a tiny campfire
that I put out as soon as we eaten. Without being asked, Willie
washed the utensils in the creek.

"Yer bein' awful careful, Mr. Tackett," Willie said.

"Ya never know who's out there," I replied. "No use in callin' attention to ourselves."

We turned in soon after that and, as usual, I slept with one ear
cocked and woke up a half dozen times during the night. But it
passed quiet enough except for a couple of coyotes howling in the
distance. I shook Willie awake at dawn and less than an hour later we
were back on the trail. We'd run out of food and coffee the night
before and I was in a hurry to get to Cutbank and get a square meal,
maybe even a couple of fried eggs.

A mile on down the road, Willie spotted a plume of smoke off to
the left.

"Bet there's a ranchhouse on the other side of that rise," he said.

"Let's take a look," I said. "Mebbe they got a spare cup of real coffee."

We'd been seeing more and more cattle but hadn't got close
enough to read a brand. They were mostly white-faced Herefords—
a stocky breed that was getting more and more popular—and they
were filling out nice on the late summer grass.

We cantered over the rise and there, nestled against the side of
another low hill, was one of the neatest little spreads you'd ever want
to see. The house was one-story and small, three or at the most four

rooms. It was painted white with red shutters on the windows and a red door. The barn was as big as the house, but taller and unpainted. It looked to be in good condition, and there was a sturdy looking corral with a half dozen horses in it.

As we got closer I spotted a kitchen garden off to the left and flower beds on both sides of the steps that led up to a covered porch running corner to corner across the front of the house.

"Looks like carin' folk live here," Willie remarked.

"I hope they care fer strangers," I said.

There was a small hitching rail about ten yards from the porch and a path outlined by painted white rocks leading from it to the front steps.

I was starting to dismount when Willie said, "Mr. Tackett!" in a tight, low voice. I settled back down in the saddle. "What is it, Willie?"

"Them horses in the corral. A couple of 'em look familiar."

"Let's take a look-see," I said.

We reined around and cantered over to the corral.

"There." Willie pointed. "See that Rockin' W? That's one of old man Websterby's brands."

"Well, dang," I said, as usual remembering Ma's aversion to cussing. "How do ya suppose they got here ahead of us?"

"Somethin' I can do for you fellers?" a strange voice said.

I looked up and saw a white-haired man with pale blue eyes set wide apart in a square face walking toward us from the barn.

He was wearing blue jeans and a blue denim shirt and carrying a milk bucket, but as far as I could see he wasn't carrying no gun.

"We was hopin' for a cup of coffee," I said. "But it looks like you got company so we won't bother ya none."

"No bother," he said. "Coffee's made. So's breakfast. Light and come on in."

"Yeah. Light and come on in," another voice said, this one comin' from the direction of the house.

I looked over to see who'd spoke and danged if it wasn't von Cart. He was pointing his six-shooter at us as he walked out the door and across the porch to the front steps.

"Let's go, Willie," I yelled and I jabbed my spurs into Old Dobbin's flanks. Surprised and hurt, he taken off at a full gallop, with Willie's crowbait pinto right behind. I heard shots fired and I ducked but no bullet come near me. Looking back at Willie, though, I saw the pinto stagger. I reined Old Dobbin in and he fell back to where he was running even with the pinto, then I reached out an arm and grabbed Willie out of the saddle just as the pinto stumbled and went down.

I dragged Old Dobbin to a halt, let Willie swing up behind me, and then we were off and running back the way we'd come. It'd take them a few minutes to saddle up and come after us and I figured by then we'd be back at the creek and maybe we could lose them—or at least confuse them for a while.

By the time we got to the creek Old Dobbin begun to slow up noticeable. I rode him into the middle of the creek where me and Willie dismounted. Then we walked upstream leaving footprints in the sandy bottom that I hoped would wash away before von Cart and the rest of the Websterby crew arrived.

I'd heard that almost any time a feller goes into a stream to try to lose whoever's following him, he comes out on the same side of the stream he went in. So a hundred yards up the creek we went out on the opposite side. I stopped and brushed out our tracks the best I could and scattered some leaves around, knowing it wouldn't fool a real good tracker very long but figuring it might buy us a little time.

In back of us now I heard some shouting; von Cart's folks had got to the stream. We taken off at a fast walk upstream, weaving in and out amongst the trees, me and Willie on foot and me leading Old Dobbin.

"Mebbe we oughta stay and fight 'em," Willie said, panting a little from the fast walk.

"Sometimes it's better to run, Willie," I said drily. "And this here is one of them times."

"We could sure use another horse," he whined.

"Ya fergot to teach yer pinto how to duck," I said.

We came to a place where the stream narrowed as it flowed through a cut in a low hill. I could see an overgrown stream bed where water had flowed around the hill for generations before finally slicing its way through it. After a short hesitation I led Old Dobbin into the stream and the three of us headed into the cut, walking single file.

Ten minutes later as we walked out of the cut and into the open, a voice said, "Stop right there you all and don't move."

I stopped where I stood and the voice said, "Sonny, you move your hand an inch nearer your gun and you won't have a hand left to move."

I snuck a glance over at Willie. "Don't be a damn fool, kid. He's got the drop."

"Put your hands on top of your heads and come on out of the water," the voice said. "You, there. You can lead the horse out, but keep your other hand in the air."

As Willie and me stepped on dry land, a tall old man with a grizzled grey beard and grey hair stepped from behind a huge sycamore tree. He was wearing buckskin pants and a fringed buckskin pullover shirt. He wore a six-gun on his right hip and in his left hand he carried a double-barrelled shotgun. I stared at him and it came to me that he looked kind of familiar, like I'd seen him somewheres before.

"You ain't one of them?" I said

"Whoever 'them' are I'm not one of them," he said agreeably. There was just the trace of a drawl in his voice like some folks I'd known around the West who'd fought for the South in the War Between the States.

"Mister," I said, "I don't know who you are but 'them' is a bunch of old man Websterby's men from down Kolakoka way. They're mebbe ten minutes behind us and if they catch us they'll shoot us or hang us. They got a lawman with 'em, too. He's not a bad old man but he's bought and paid for by Websterby."

"Websterby," the stranger said. "That's an unusual name. Would that by any chance be Tod Websterby?"

"Yep."

"That being the case, I'll help you," he said. "Follow me."

The old man was wearing moccasins and I wished I could take a minute and switch into mine, but I figured we needed to put as much distance as possible as quick as possible between us and the Websterby folks.

The old man moved at an easy lope, following the thread of a trail that ran alongside the stream. After a few minutes he stopped to listen and I taken advantage of the stop to switch into my moccasins.

I looked at Willie and he looked pretty beat. He was breathing hard.

"You climb on board Old Dobbin," I said.

He shook his head. "I'm all right."

"Don't argue," I said. "Mount up."

"I don't hear anything," the old man said. "If they're coming they're back a ways."

I noticed he wasn't even taking a deep breath.

"It's not much farther," he said.

A few minutes later, where the stream was skirting another hill, he stopped again, this time where a dry, brush-filled wash ran down the hillside to the creek. Without saying a word he went back a ways, scattering leaves and dirt to hide our tracks.

"We'll cross here," he said when he came back. The stream was only a few feet wide, but it was running swiftly. On the other side, he pulled back the branches of a large bush that grew down to the water's edge, and gestured to Willie and me to go past it and up the wash that the bush had hidden.

We waited on the other side of the bush whilst he wiped out our tracks again. Then he let go of the bush's branches and they sprang back into place, completely hiding the entry to the wash.

He led the way up the steep slope of the wash and I followed, holding on to Old Dobbin's reins while Willie, who'd dismounted again, brought up the rear. At the top we came out on a pretty little mesa, no more than five or six acres, backed up against the side of a higher hill. That high hill had been hidden from our sight by the side of the lower hill we'd just climbed.

There were trees growing back against the hillside and on up the slope but the mesa was mainly lush grass. A small herd of Herefords, maybe fifty head, grazed quietly, and I saw that the one closest to us was wearing a Double-B-Connected brand. As I looked around I spotted a house amongst the trees, an easy rifle-shot distance from where we was. As we came closer, I noticed a small barn next to the house and a corral next to that. In the corral were two tall and sturdy horses, each one fit to carry easy the man who had led us here. I unsaddled Old Dobbin and turned him into the corral, then headed for the house where Willie and the old man were waiting for me.

The house was an odd mixture of stone and logs and cut lumber, but it was sturdily built and commanded a view of the whole mesa. From the looks of it, the stone part was older than the rest and the stones had been fit close together by someone who must of been a master stone mason.

The old man pushed open the heavy wooden front door and stood aside as me and Willie entered.

"This is home," he said. "If they find their way onto the mesa here, this is where we'll make our stand."

"There's gotta be another way in and out," I said.

"There is."

"Best thing for Willie and me—and fer you too, as far as that goes—is fer you to show it to us and let us get out of here. I ain't about to bring our troubles down on yer head."

"Perhaps you're right," he said. "I don't mind a fight, but I'd just as soon not call too much attention to myself or my place. It's quiet and peaceful here and I'd like to keep it that way. Unless that happens to be the Tod Websterby I know."

He shook his head. "It can't be. No reason for him to be in this part of the country."

"Mister," I said, "me and Willie's headin' for Cutbank, which is where we was goin' when we run into trouble back there a ways. They shot Willie's pinto out from under him and I was wonderin', might you have a horse and saddle we could borrow? You know Cutbank?"

He nodded.

"There's a feller there name of Frank Honerock. Runs the newspaper. We'd leave yer horse with him."

"I know him," he said. "I'll lend you a horse and saddle. You leave them with Honerock. Take the red mare. There's a spare saddle in the barn. While you're saddling up, I'll make some coffee. I could use some and I expect you could, too."

Whilst he was talking I taken a quick look around the room. It was rough-hewn but comfortable, with cowhides for rugs on a stone floor and some bookcases along a stone wall that backed up to the side of the hill. On both sides of the front door there was narrow, shuttered windows with a good view of the mesa, windows a defender could fire out of without exposing much of himself. Between the windows on one side hung a crossed pair of cavalry swords and between the windows on the other side hung a tattered Confederate flag.

It crossed my mind that he must have fought for the South in the War Between the States and that accounted for his drawl. Well, there were a lot of former soldiers out here in the West, men who'd fought on both sides, and most of them held no grudge, not twenty-three years after Appomattox. Well, it wasn't none of my business who he was or who he'd fought for. It was enough that he was friendly and willing to help.

By the time Willie and me had finished saddling the horses, the old man was standing out in front with his rifle in one hand and a packet in the other.

"I thought you might get hungry along the way," he said, handing me the package which I stowed in my saddlebag.

"I'll show you the way out," he offered, then he kind of narrowed his eyes and stopped. "No, I won't. It's too late," he said, looking past me to the spot where we'd come up on the mesa.

Before I could move he grabbed up a rifle that was leaning on the wall next to the door and fired a shot in the direction of the spot where we come up onto the mesa.

"One of your friends," he said grimly. "I didn't try to hit him, just scare him. It'll be a while before they try coming up again."

"Mister," I said, "we seem to of brought a heap of trouble on ya."

He laughed, but it wasn't a happy sound. "My pleasure. Any enemy of Tod Websterby is a friend of mine."

"What do ya figure we do now?" I asked.

"You and the boy go on," he said. "The trail out of here is behind the barn. It heads north to Cutbank. I'll stay here. One man can hold them off the mesa until dark unless they find the other way in. If that happens—well, I have provisions in the house for a long siege."

"You come or we stay," I said. "We got ya into this fix. We ain't leavin' ya here to fight our fight fer us."

He stared at me a long time and I couldn't get over the feeling that I'd seen him somewhere before.

"Maybe you're right," he said. "There's really not much sense in staying. Eventually they'd burn me out or starve me out. Especially if that's the Websterby I know. He's a mighty mean man."

He hurried off to the corral and in a few minutes was back, riding his tall roan gelding. He dismounted, went back into the house, and came out with the tattered Confederate flag, folding it as he walked.

"Let's go," he said, stuffing the flag into a saddlebag. "I hope they don't burn the house. It's been home for a long time."

He led the way around the barn and onto a narrow trail that skirted the hill for a little ways and then took off at an angle that led through a scattering of trees along the side of the hill. The trail was narrow but was well-used, and it was plain that this was the old man's regular way in and out.

After about a mile the trail dipped back down to flat land where there were a few more white-faced cattle grazing. A near one turned so I could see the brand. It was the Double-B-Connected, the same as the cattle on the mesa. The old man signaled for us to halt and reined up.

"This joins up with the main trail a little way ahead," he said. "From there it's a straight shot to Cutbank. It's about a three-hour ride. We'll be there well before dark."

CHAPTER 9

IT WAS MID-AFTERNOON when we walked our horses down Cutbank's main street. Cutbank was a typical cowtown with a dirt main street and a few side streets. It had the usual unpainted buildings that housed a general store, at least two saloons that I could spot, a livery stable, a jail, a small church, a one-room schoolhouse, a place that said EATS, and the Cutbank *Herald,* the weekly paper run by Colonel Rankin's old friend Frank Honerock.

The man in buckskins led us to a hitching rack in front of the Grand Saloon that sat directly across the street from the *Herald* and was the only two-story building in town.

"There's no hotel here," he said. "But the Grand has a few rooms to rent. Otherwise, old Mrs. Witherspoon takes in boarders or you can bed down at the stable or under the stars, whatever suits you."

"What about you?" I asked.

"Frank Honerock usually has a bed for me."

"Honerock's the galoot I come to see," I said. "Willie and me'll see if we can get a room at the Grand, then I'll mosey on over to the paper. When ya see Honerock tell him there's a feller wants to talk to him."

Willie and me dismounted, tied our horses, and headed into the saloon while the man in buckskins reined his big roan across the street to the *Herald.*

The yella-haired bartender taken one look at me, grinned, and said, "Tackett! What in tarnation brings you to Cutbank?"

"Howdy, Swanny," I said. "Huntin' a feller. What're you doin' here? Willie, this here is John Swann. A honest bartender. We knowed each other a while back. Swanny, this here is Willie. Him and me is saddle pardners."

"Last time I seen you was in Goldarado," he said. "Three or four years back. You was ridin' shotgun on the stage. After you left, the gold petered out and so did the town. The saloon was the last place to close and after that I drifted for a while and finally lit here. You?"

"Like I said, I'm looking for a feller. After I find him me and Willie are headin' back to the Arizona Territory. I been ramroddin' a ranch down there."

While I was talking Swann set out a bottle and two glasses.

Willie looked up at me, his face red with embarrassment.

"Mr. Tackett, I ain't taken to drinkin' yet."

"Swanny," I said "Willie here don't like the stuff. You got a sarsaparilla back there?"

He nodded. "Sure enough." He brought out a bottle from under the bar, uncapped it and set it in front of Willie. "Be smart, kid," he said. "If you ain't drinkin', don't start. I never seen likker do no one any good."

"Business must be good for you to be chasin' away customers," I chuckled.

Swann grunted. "Good enough."

"Feller said you got rooms to rent," I said.

"Upstairs," he said. "The two front ones are vacant. Take yer pick."

"Me and Willie'll each take a room," I said.

I turned to Willie. "Willie, I need a hand. I'd be mighty grateful if you'd take our gear to our rooms and then take the horses to the stable and rub 'em down. I got business across the street. When I'm done I'll join ya at the stable or meet ya back here."

Willie shuffled his feet but didn't say nothing. I reached in my pocket and pulled out a couple of coins. "Here," I said. "This'll take care of the horses."

Looking relieved, Willie took the coins and headed out the batwing doors. I followed him, ducked under the hitch rail, and walked across the street to the *Herald* building. The door was open so I walked in.

Inside a pretty young woman with yellow hair and a full figure was sitting at a desk behind a wooden counter that looked like it could double for a bar except that it didn't have a foot-rail.

She looked up in time to catch me eyeing her. I could see the color coming into her cheeks, but she looked square at me—defiant, I thought.

"Can I help you with something?" she asked coolly.

Under my three-days growth of beard I could feel my ownself blushing.

"Didn't mean to be starin', ma'am," I said, fumbling with my hat. "But it ain't often you find a pretty girl in a backwater town like this."

"Mr. Whatever-your-name-is, you didn't come here to discuss my looks. What is it you wanted?"

"Dang," I said. "I sure seem to have got off on a wrong foot. I'm truly sorry, ma'am. Ma taught me better than to be rude. Maybe you could help me. I come here lookin' for Mr. Honerock—Frank Honerock."

She smiled unexpectedly. "It's miss, not ma'am, and your apology is accepted. Mr. Honerock has gone to the restaurant with an old friend. He will be back in about an hour."

"Was that an old feller wearin' buckskins?" I asked.

"Why, yes. Is he a friend of yours, too?"

"Not hardly. But he saved my bacon earlier today so you might say I got me a friendly feelin' for him."

"Well, I'm sure Mr. Honerock wouldn't object if you joined them. They've gone down to the Cutbank Cafe, the one with the sign that says 'Eats.' When you go outside, turn right. It's just a little way down. You can't miss it."

"Thanks a heap, miss, " I said, putting my hat back on and turning to go.

I taken one step outside and ducked right back in, closing the door behind me. The girl looked up with a question on her face.

"There's some folks out there I think have come lookin' for me. And if they are who I think they are, they ain't my friends. Ya got a back door here?"

"Yes, we do, but if you wish you can wait here until they're gone or until Uncle Frank returns," she said, and the look on her face turned from questioning to concern.

"That's mighty kind of ya, Miss," I said. "But that's a mean bunch out there and I wouldn't want to get you and Mr. Honerock in trouble. So I'll just be duckin' out the back way."

I headed for the back door at a run, past the old Washington flatbed printing press, the California job case, and the stacks of newsprint that Frank Honerock had carted in from somewhere. The door was locked shut with a heavy hook-and-eye latch. I flipped the hook out of the eye, opened the door, and taken a quick look around. There was no one in sight.

Once outside I walked quick along the back of the buildings toward the restaurant. I wasn't looking for nothing to eat, but I remembered that the stranger who had befriended me and Willie also seemed to be an enemy of Tod Websterby and I didn't want him getting caught with his pants down, so to speak. I hadn't gone very far when I spotted a man standing at a back door, throwing out a dish pan full of water.

I stopped. "Frank Honerock in there?"

"Yep," he said, and I brushed by him, ignoring his startled look.

I spotted the man in buckskins right off. He was sitting at a table with a tall old man with a beak nose and a fringe of white hair. In his black broadcloth suit, white shirt, and string tie, he could of passed for an undertaker. They spotted me at the same time and looked at me curiously as I went up to them.

"Mister," I said to the man in buckskins, "if I'm right and I think I am, Tod Websterby and his men are in town."

He nodded calmly. "Thanks. I appreciate that. I'll deal with him if he comes in here."

"Well, I'll be danged," I said. "I figured—"

Frank Honerock interrupted me. "There won't be any trouble here," he said. "That man across the room is the sheriff and he's used to handling men like Websterby."

"Mr. Honerock," I said, "that's a mighty tough bunch out there."

"We appreciate your warning, Mr.—?"

Before I could answer, the door was thrown open and a man who had to be Tod Websterby hisself burst into the room, followed by five armed men who crowded in behind him.

This was the first time I had gotten a look at Websterby. He was about the same age as Honerock and his friend. He wasn't very big, kind of scrawny in fact, with a shock of grey hair, bushy grey eyebrows over pale blue eyes set deep in his head, and a mean look on his narrow, pinched face. He was wearing range clothes and carried a six-shooter on his left hip, butt forward.

"That's him, Boss," one of his men said, pointing at me. I'd turned and faced them with my hand ready over my gun butt and I recognized the man who spoke as one of them who was with Bailey Harbor. But Websterby wasn't looking at me. Instead he was staring at the man in buckskins, who had gotten to his feet.

"Well, I'll be damned," Websterby spit out. "You. It's you. I'd have recognized you anywhere."

"It's me, you scum. After all these years, it's me," the man in buckskin said in a quiet voice. "And now that you've found me, I'm going to kill you."

"Sit down, BeeBee. Ain't nobody killin' nobody in my town," a voice from the side said.

I turned and looked. A heavy-set man, black-haired and tough-looking, with a star pinned on his vest, stepped between the man in buckskins—the one he called BeeBee—and Websterby.

"You," he said to Websterby. "I don't know you and I don't know what yer doin' here. But you start any trouble in my town and I'll throw you in jail and keep you there 'til hell freezes over." He turned to BeeBee. "And that goes fer you, too."

Honerock stood up and threw a silver dollar on the table. "Come on, BeeBee, let's get out of here," he said, heading for the kitchen and the back door. "You can deal with Mr. Websterby some other time."

The man in buckskin followed him, but stopped at the kitchen door and spoke to Websterby. "I meant what I said, Major. You stay around this part of the country and I'll kill you."

He turned and vanished into the kitchen.

Immediately Websterby turned to the sheriff. "Sheriff, that man there"—he nodded at me—"is an escaped prisoner. He was being held for rustling my cows down in the Kolakoka country on the Sun River. I want him."

The sheriff looked at me. "That true, Mister?"

I nodded. "They was gonna lynch me, Sheriff. The sheriff down there is in their pocket. He went off and left the jail unlocked fer 'em. His deputy turned me loose and we headed up here. I'm lookin' fer a feller."

"He's lying, Sheriff. He was changing the brand on one of my steers," Websterby protested. "We caught him at it and we damn sure aim to teach him a lesson." He laughed mirthlessly. "His last lesson."

"You got a warrant for his arrest?" the sheriff asked.

"No, I don't have a warrant for his arrest. I'm following an escaped prisoner. I want you to hold this man until the sheriff of Kolakoka gets here. He'll be here in an hour or so."

The sheriff looked at me. "Seems like that's a reasonable request."

I looked at the sheriff. Then I looked at Websterby and the five hard-looking men with him. I was between a rock and a hard place and I knew it. If I surrendered I knew for sure the sheriff would turn me over to Websterby, and if he did that I was a dead duck. They'd hang me to the first tree as soon as they got out of sight of town. And von Cart wouldn't lift a finger to stop them.

On the other hand, if I tried to escape now they'd shoot me down like a dog before I got fifty feet. Still, that was better than hanging. And I knew one thing for sure. I'd get my gun out and get off at least one shot, and the man I'd aim at would be Tod Websterby.

The sheriff read my mind. "Don't try it, son," he advised. "You better gimme yer gun."

"I'm a dead man if I do, Sheriff."

"Yer a dead man if ya don't."

As I hesitated, a shot rang out from the cafe entrance and a young voice yelled, "First man who moves is a dead man!"

It was Willie.

"Take off, Tackett," he shouted. "We'll hold 'em."

"We?" I asked.

"Me and Botrish and his injuns," he called. "Get goin'."

Without thinking, I wheeled and ran into the kitchen and out the back door. Behind me I heard three shots close together, then silence. Turning to my right I ran until I recognized the back of the *Herald* building. I opened the door and ducked inside.

I stopped, breathing hard and realizing that I had panicked. It wasn't like me, but I had. It was Willie did it. Offering me a chance at freedom when I had known I was a dead man, and I'd taken it without thinking about the consequences. I should have drawed my gun and stayed to help. Why didn't I?

I didn't have an answer. I knew I wasn't going to surrender. I wasn't going to let old Tod Websterby hang me, but I didn't want to kill that sheriff. He seemed like a good man. So when Willie told me to run, I ran.

Dang! That was a fool thing to do. Now I had to get back there and see how it was going with Willie and Botrish and his Indians. See what I could do to help.

I turned again and started to open the back door when I heard a voice say, "Where do ya reckon he went?"

They were out there hunting for me. Any second they might start opening back doors, including this one. The light was dim where I was standing but I felt around and found the heavy hook- and-eye latch. I put the hook into the eye that was screwed into the door, then stepped toward the office at the front of the building.

The jingle of my spurs stopped me. I reached down, took off my boots, and tiptoed toward the front. I hadn't taken but a few steps when a woman's voice—I took it to be the blonde girl's—called, "Is that you, Uncle Frank?"

I stopped in my tracks, holding my breath, and I heard her chair scrape as she pushed it back and stood up. Her heels echoed on the plank floor as she headed toward me and I could see her figure silhouetted against the front window.

"Miss," I said in low voice, "it's just me. The feller who was here a little while ago. They're huntin' me out there, includin' yer sheriff. I'd be mighty grateful if you'd make like I wasn't here."

"Was that you shooting a little bit ago?" she asked.

"No, ma'am. That was Willie, my saddle pardner. And I think he's in trouble. Soon as things quiet down I got to see if he is."

Before she could say anything I heard the front door open and a voice that sounded like Honerock's called, "Annabelle? You here?"

"I'm here, Uncle Frank," she called back. "I'll be right with you."

To me she whispered, "You hide behind those stacks of paper and I'll see what's going on."

I ducked behind the stacks of paper and she turned and went into the office. I could hear the low murmur of voices and then I heard the front door open and close.

Dang, I said to myself. They've went for the sheriff.

Quicklike I hurried to the back door. I shoved my feet into my boots, flicked the hook out of the eye, opened the door just wide enough to get out, stood there a second or two to get accustomed to the light, then drawed my gun and stepped outside.

CHAPTER 10

THE MID-AFTERNOON sun was still shining brightly but the back of the building where I stood looking around was in shadow. The two men searching for me were nowhere to be seen.

A hundred yards beyond the rear of the building was a line of brush and scrub trees that I was pretty sure bordered a small stream. I thought about making a dash for it, but decided against it. That was one place they'd be sure to look for me, even if I got there without anyone spotting me. I scratched my head, trying to figure out my next step. A bench by the back door caught my eye and gave me an idea.

If I stood on the bench, the edge of the roof would be only about six inches out of my reach. I remembered that the *Herald* building, like many others in the ramshackle towns of the West, had a false front and a flat roof. If I could get on the roof without being seen, I could hunker down in the shadow of that false front and wait 'til dark.

I didn't hesitate. I stepped onto the bench, jumped, and caught the edge of the roof with my fingertips. I pulled myself up 'til I could get one elbow on the roof and then the other. After that it was easy. I swang my right foot onto the roof and then just kind of rolled myself onto it.

No sooner was I up there than the back door opened and the girl named Annabelle called softly, "Are you there?"

I didn't answer and after a minute she went back inside. I crawled as quiet as I could over the hot tarpaper roof 'til I reached the shade of the false front. I thought about peeking over to see what was going on but thought better of it. Anybody saw me up there, I'd be a dead duck.

I didn't hear any sound to indicate that Honerock had come back with the sheriff, so maybe I was wrong but I wasn't going to take no chances. I'd never be able to help Willie and Zell Botrish—if he'd really joined up with Willie—if I was dead or in jail.

When there's nothing to be done, sometimes it's better to do nothing. And that's just what I did. I laid down in the shade of that false front, put my hat over my eyes, and went to sleep. When I woke up the sun was down and it was turning dark.

I got up carefully and stuck my nose over the top of the false front to look up and down the street. Lamplight was shining through the open doors of the Grand Saloon and of another saloon a few doors down. Here and there you could see lights in the windows of houses and cabins and stores. On beyond the main street was another street, and at one end of it a half a dozen red lanterns glowed. The ladies of the evening were open for business.

A few people were still on the street, and I watched a couple of cowboys rein up in front of the other saloon. Then I tiptoed to the back of the building and scrambled on down to the ground. As I did, I noticed a ladder propped against the building on the far side of the doorway. Dang! I hadn't noticed that when I climbed onto the roof a couple of hours back. In fact, I was sure it wasn't there then.

Somebody had put that ladder there whilst I was sleeping. If whoever it was was looking for me he'd of seen me. Even if he wasn't after me, he'd of been hard put to miss me. That meant whoever it was wasn't one of Websterby's men. I thought about it, and it seemed to me it had to of been Frank Honerock. Or maybe that blonde girl who worked in his office. His niece, I guessed. Leastways, she called him "Uncle Frank."

I tried the back door and it opened easily and silently. Inside, I could see the glow of a light at the front of the building. Just as I started to tiptoe toward it, a voice off to one side said, "Been waiting for you, Mister. It's all right. I'm friendly. I thought you might come in after you saw the ladder."

I stopped dead still. "That you, Mr. Honerock?"

"You guessed right, Mister," he said.

"I need to talk to ya."

He gave a dry chuckle. "I'm not surprised. "Between the sheriff and Tod Websterby you're in a lot of trouble. Tell you what. I'll go lock up and then we can go to my place and talk. I don't think anyone will be looking for you there."

We had just begun walking toward the front when the front door burst open and a voice shouted, "Yo! Honerock!"

"I'm here," he replied. For the second time in about a minute I stopped dead in my tracks. But Honerock kept on walking.

"You hidin' that rustler I want?" a voice I thought to be Websterby's demanded.

"I'm the only one here, Mr. Websterby," Honerock answered. "We'll see about that," Websterby snarled. "Get in here, men. We're gonna search this place."

"Don't move, Mr. Websterby," Honerock said calmly. "I have a gun aimed at you and you're silhouetted plainly against the light. If you don't take your men and leave, you're dead."

There was a long silence. "Leave. Now," Honerock said, still not raising his voice.

"I'm goin'," Websterby said spitefully. "But if I find out you been hidin' that fella I'll be back and I'll tear this place down."

"Goodnight, Mr. Websterby," Honerock said.

He waited until Websterby had left, slamming the door behind him, then went and locked it.

He came back to where I was standing. "That was a little scary," he said. "I was running a bluff. I don't carry a gun."

"I do, Mr. Honerock," I said. "And it was pointed right at him. I couldn't see who he was but I could sure see where he was and you was right. If he hadn't of left when ya told him to he'd of been a dead man."

"You're a good man, Mister——" He stopped. "Son, I don't even know your name. Not that it matters, of course."

"I'm proud to tell ya, Mr. Honerock," I said. "It's Tackett. William Delligan Tackett. Only you can call me Del."

"Tackett!" He almost shouted it. "Come on, boy—Del. We do have a lot to talk about." He stepped around in front of me and headed for the back door with me right on his heels. "Tackett," I heard him say. "Well, I'll be damned."

He opened the back door and stepped outside. I saw him jerk and go down at the same time I heard the roar of the guns. I couldn't tell how many, but I was sure there was at least three of them.

Without thinking, I dropped to the floor, drawing my six-shooter and rolling over against the wall all in the same motion. Through the open door I could hears spurs jingling as the gunmen walked up to Honerock's body.

"He dead?" one asked.

"As a doornail." It was Tod Websterby's voice and in my mind's eye I could see him nudging Honerock's body with his boot.

A light flared as someone struck a match. "Boss, it ain't Tackett," a third voice said.

"Well, it doesn't much matter," Websterby said. "This fella had it comin', talkin' to me the way he did. Come daylight we'll find Tackett. He's not goin' anywhere without us knowin' about it. Come on, let's get the men out in front and head for camp."

"What about gettin' a drink o' whiskey first, Boss?"

"Not tonight," Websterby said. "I don't want that sheriff seein' any of us hangin' around town. Old man Honerock's a big wheel here and I don't want the town turnin' on us. Tomorrow, maybe, when we're through with Tackett."

Their voices faded as they walked away.

I waited 'til I was sure they were gone, then cautiously I stepped outside. I looked down at the body of Frank Honerock, who'd seemed to be a fine old man, and I was mad clean through. He'd taken a bullet or bullets meant for me. I looked around, wondering what to do. I knew I couldn't leave him lying there.

Then I thought I heard a groan. I stood real still, hardly breathing, and sure enough, there was another groan. Honerock was still alive.

It was dark and I couldn't see how bad he was hurt, but I figured with at least three guns shooting at him he had to of been shot to doll rags.

I bent over him. "Mr. Honerock. You conscious?"

There was no answer.

Making a quick decision, I bent over and picked him up in my arms like you'd cradle a baby. He was a tall old man, but lean and not as heavy as I'd thought he'd be. My plan was to take him inside and lay him down up in the front office, then take my chances and see if I could find a doctor. The odds were against there being a doctor in a town the size of Cutbank, but I had to try.

I was just stepping inside the back door when a woman's voice that sounded like Honerock's niece called low, "Uncle Frank? Is that you?"

"No, ma'am," I said as she came near. "Yer uncle's been shot. I was just takin' him inside afore I went huntin' a doctor."

I heard her gasp. "You shot him!" she accused.

"No, Miss, it weren't me. It was Websterby and his gang. They bushwhacked him as he was comin' out the door here. They thought it was me. He's bad hurt. We got to get him somewhere where we can see where's he been hit. We got to stop the bleedin' quick."

"Can you carry him to our house?"

"Miss, I can carry him as far as I have to."

Without another word she started off almost running toward a light I could see shining maybe two hundred yards away. I followed behind with Frank Honerock in my arms. When we reached the house I trailed her up the porch steps and inside. She grabbed the lit lamp and with me at her heels hurried down a hallway to a back bedroom where there was a big old hand-carved wooden bedstead, thick with mattresses.

"The princess could of slept here," I murmured, laying him softly on top of the coverlet and gently straightening him out.

"What was that you said?" she asked.

"Nothin', Miss."

This was no time to tell her—nor I wouldn't have anyway—that me, a grown man near thirty years old, had only recently learned to read. For the last nearly a year I'd been reading everything I could get my hands on. Right now there were two books in my saddlebags that I had brung along from the R-Bar-R. One of them was a book of fairy tales that had this story about a princess and a pea and how, because she was a real princess, the lady in the story couldn't sleep on account of she could feel a dried pea under a whole bunch of mattresses. Well, there wasn't no pea under Frank Honerock's mattresses that I knew of, but there were growing bloodstains on the coverlet.

"We got to get his clothes off and see where he's shot," I said.

She looked up at me from where she was leaning over her uncle. "Oh, God! You've been shot, too."

I looked down and saw that my shirt and vest were covered with blood.

"That's from yer uncle," I said. "You get me some clean cloths and get some water to boilin' whilst I get his clothes off. You got a doctor in town?"

"There's a man who calls himself a doctor, but he doesn't have an office and he's usually intoxicated."

"Better'n nothin'," I said. "Put on the water, get me some cloths, and go find him."

She scooted out of the room and was back in a few seconds with a cotton sheet that she quickly tore into squares, then folded into pads.

In the meantime I had taken off the old man's coat, vest, and tie and unbuttoned his shirt. From the looks of him Websterby and his men hadn't missed him much, but because he was standing sideways to them when they fired, the bullets hadn't hit him head on. One bullet had gouged a furrow along his forehead. He'd been shot twice in the right arm. And one bullet looked like it had gone through his arm and into his side. Another one looked to have hit him in the side, glanced off a rib, and come out his back.

There was blood on his trousers, too, and when I pulled them and his long johns down I could see two bullet holes in his right thigh. When I looked closer I was glad he was an old man.

One of the wounds in his arm was still pumping blood and I guessed a bullet must of hit an artery. I tore one of the pads into strips and used them to tie another pad tight around his arm to stop the flow of blood.

He was beginning to groan now, and I looked at his face. It was white and his lips were bloodless. Right then I wouldn't of bet a lot on his chances.

I ran into the kitchen, found the kettle of hot water, and carried it into the bedroom. Soaking a pad, I cleaned his wounds the best I could and bound them up.

Just then the front door opened and I heard footsteps hurrying down the hall. I pulled the half of the coverlet Honerock wasn't lying on over his legs and waist as Annabelle came into the room, all breathless and upset.

"I found him," she gasped. "He's gone to get his bag. He said he'll be right over."

She looked at her uncle, shivered, and turned away. "He's dying, isn't he?"

"I don't know, Miss," I said. "He's bad hurt but he's a tough old man. Dang! Where's that doctor?" I looked right at her then and made a promise. "I'll tell you one thing Miss—Annabelle, isn't it? I will get the men who did this. I swear I will."

"Oh, please," she said, "I don't want any more violence."

I stared at her. "Miss, if someone doesn't stop those men they'll go on killin' anyone who gets in their way."

She didn't say anything—not that she agreed with me or didn't—and turned away. A loud knock on the front door stopped any more talk and she hurried out of the room to answer it. She came back almost pushing another tall, skinny old man, even taller than me, in front of her.

He had sparse grey hair, a beak of a nose, pale blue eyes set deep, and a dirty mustache over thin lips and a prominent chin. His nose and sunken cheeks were red-veined, but he seemed sober. He was clutching a black satchel in one hand.

He taken one look at Frank Honerock. "I don't think I can do anything here," he said in a deep, gravelly voice.

"Mister," I growled, forgetting Ma's dislike of swearing, "you had damn well better try."

He shrugged and set his satchel on the edge of the bed.

"Go boil some more water, Miss," he said, looking with disdain at the blood-stained water in the kettle. When she was gone, he threw back the coverlet.

"Bad as it looks?" he asked softly.

"Yep."

"Well, go get the water and tell her to stay out of here until I say she can come in. Then you come back and help me."

"Do yer best, Doc. He's a good old man," I said and went out, looking for the kitchen.

An hour later he straighted up and stretched. "I've done all I can do," he said. "It's a miracle he's still alive. He's lost a lot of blood and he's in deep shock. We need to get some liquids in him—tea would be good—and after that it's up to the Lord."

"Doc," I said, "can you stay the night? It'd help."

"I can," he said. "But a drink would be mighty helpful."

I went to the door and opened it to find Annabelle waiting right outside.

"The doc thinks we should try to get your uncle to drink some tea. And the doc, he could use somethin' stronger."

"I'll be right back," she said and hurried away again. She came back with a fancy-shaped glass bottle.

"It's brandy," she said. "It's what Uncle Frank drinks. And here's a glass. I'll go make the tea."

I handed the bottle and glass to the doctor and he filled the glass half full. He looked at it longingly but didn't drink any. "Let's try to get a little of this down Mr. Honerock," he said.

I lifted Honerock's head and the doc poured a little of the brandy into his mouth. Honerock gave a slight cough and opened his eyes.

"It hurts," he said, and sank back, closing his eyes again.

The doctor straighted up, lifted the glass, raised his eyes to the ceiling, said, "It's up to *you* now," and downed the drink. Then he refilled the glass and downed it again. "That's better," he said, smacking his thin lips. "You better take it away now. I don't want to be tempted. After we get a little tea into him, I'll sleep in the chair here."

In a few minutes Annabelle came in with the tea and we lifted the old man up again and poured some down him, which luckily he swallowed without choking.

"I'll be spending the night here, Miss," the doc told Annabelle. "So don't worry. If there's anything needs doing I'll do it. Oh, and by the way, let me introduce myself. I'm Doctor Barry Marien, late of our nation's capital and other parts East. And once," he added, "I was a very good surgeon."

"Tackett," I said, holding out my hand. "Del Tackett, from the high sierras and other parts West." We shook hands.

"And I'm Annabelle Owensmith, Mr. Honerock's niece, and I'm grateful to both of you."

I followed her out the door and into the parlor. "Will he live?" she asked.

"I don't know, Miss. He's bad hurt. Doc says it's a miracle he's still alive."

Tears welled up in her eyes. "He must live. He's all I've got," she said, her voice trembling.

I picked up my hat. "I'd better be goin', Miss. I'll drop back in the morning if Websterby's not huntin' me."

"Please," she said. "Couldn't you stay the night? You could have my bedroom and I could sleep on the sofa."

I hesitated only a few seconds. I had no place to stay except the room above the saloon, which right now didn't seem like a very safe place. Even though Websterby and his men were supposed to be heading for their camp, it was still possible that they might be hunting me out there in the dark. But it didn't seem likely they'd be looking for me here.

"I'll stay, Miss," I said. "But I'll sleep out here on the couch if you'll just fetch me a blanket."

CHAPTER 11

I'M A BIG man, six feet two inches in my stocking feet, and that couch was too short by half. But I draped my feet over the arm at the end of it and slept the sleep of the dead, that tired I was. It had been a long day, with Websterby and his men chasing me and Willie most of the time. Willie! Dang! What had happened to him after he sprung me loose from that tight spot at the restaurant? I'd been so busy looking after my own hide he'd plum slipped my mind. And what about Zell and Clara Botrish? Thinking about Willie and them I went to sleep.

When I woke up, it was broad daylight, which surprised me because I'm usually up at the crack of dawn. I was stiff from sleeping on that too-small sofa, but otherwise was feeling rested. I'd needed that sleep.

I heard noises coming from the kitchen and I headed that way without bothering to put on my boots. The kitchen was a big one in the corner of the house. Windows on the two outside walls made it light and cheerful. There was a fire in the cookstove and I could smell coffee. Annabelle was up and dressed and bustling around. Doc Marien was sitting at a long kitchen table sipping from a mug of hot coffee. Like me, he needed a shave and some cleaning up. Unlike me, from the trembling of his hands holding the coffee mug, it looked like he needed a drink, too.

"How is he?" I asked him first thing.

"He made it through the night. He's a tough old bird."

"Is he gonna make it?" I asked, slumping into a chair.

Annabelle put a mug of steaming coffee in front of me and answered for the doctor. "He will if my prayers mean anything."

"Certainly they can't hurt," Marien said.

I taken a swallow of the coffee. It was hot and black and tasted good.

"Wisht we was in Abilene," I said. "I know a preacher down there who could pray for him."

Annabelle looked at me with just a hint of disapproval on her face. "The Lord hears all of our prayers."

"What do ya think, Doc?" I said to Marien.

"About the Lord hearing our prayers?" he asked with just a trace of a smile.

"About Mr. Honerock makin' it."

"It's too early to tell. He's still not awake, but his color is better and he doesn't seem to be running much of a fever. We've got to get some nourishment into him and hope that infection doesn't set in."

"I'm making some soup now," Annabelle said. "And I'll have some hotcakes ready for you gentlemen in just a moment."

"That's very thoughtful of you, Miss Owensmith," the doctor said, "but I must be getting along. I'll drop in this afternoon to check on the patient and change the dressings on his wounds."

He got up to leave and I said, "Let me walk out with ya, Doc." To Annabelle I said, "You can begin cookin' them hotcakes. I'll be right back."

At the front door I stopped Marien. "What about that one wound, Doc?"

"It's not his worst one," he said. "Especially at his age. I'm worried mainly about him losing so much blood, and it's a terrible shock to a person's system to be shot as many times as he was."

"I know," I said drily.

He nodded. "I expect anyone named Sackett has been shot more than once."

"I ain't no Sackett, Doc." I said. "Name is Tackett."

"Oh, Tackett," he said. "That's interesting. There's an old-timer named Tackett who lives on a ranch out of town a ways. Are you related?"

"Don't know, Doc," I said. "That's what I come here to find out."

"I wish you luck," he said, turning and going out the door.

I stopped in the sitting room to put on my boots, then went back to the kitchen and sat down at the table.

"I put a pan with hot water in it outside the kitchen door," Annabelle said pointedly. "There's soap there, too, and Uncle Frank's razor if you'd like to shave."

Under my whiskers I felt my face turning red. I'd had so much on my mind I'd forgot all about how I looked. I stood up so quick I tipped my chair over backward. Turning to pick it up, I dropped it on the floor and fell on top of it and then slid off to one side. Behind me I heard what I thought was a giggle. I got my hands under me, pushed myself to my feet, picked up the chair, and set it back at the table.

"I'll be gettin' cleaned up," I said, not looking at her.

With my head down and my neck red with embarrassment, I went out the kitchen door. Outside next to the door I found a warped and unpainted wooden table. On it was a chipped enamel pan filled with steaming hot water. There was a dish with a bar of soap in it and a straight razor that I took to be Honerock's. I hoped he'd stropped it recent. A mirror was tacked on the wall of the house above the table, and next to it a clean towel hung on a nail.

The razor was sharp and in less than five minutes I had washed my face, shaved off nearly a week's growth of beard, and combed my hair as best I could with my fingers. What I saw in that mirror as I cleaned up wasn't much. My dark brown hair was long and shaggy and I needed a haircut bad. There was a streak of white hair along the right side of my head where a bullet had plowed a furrow a while back. There was another scar on my left cheek, a souvenir of that knife fight down on the Texas border and even without it I wouldn't have seen no raving beauty in that mirror. I buttoned up my shirt and went back in the kitchen.

Annabelle had set the table and refilled my coffee mug.

There was a platterful of pancakes sitting in front of my plate, a big pat of butter off to one side, and a pitcher that was brimful with honey. But there was no Annabelle.

I figured she wouldn't want me to wait and let them pancakes get cold and all so I dug right in. I was on about my fourth mouthful when she came back into the kitchen. I quick swallowed what I had in my mouth and stood up. She looked me over carefully for a moment.

"You look much nicer," she smiled.

I felt my face redden again. Dang that girl! She had a knack for making me feel foolish. "Thank you, ma'am," I said.

"Please sit down and finish eating." she said. "The sheriff came by while you were washing up. He said Doctor Marien told him Uncle Frank had been shot and he wanted to see him. I said Uncle Frank was still sleeping, and in any event wouldn't be able to talk to him until tomorrow at the earliest. He also asked if I had seen you. He doesn't want to arrest you, but he said if I saw you to tell you he had your friend in jail."

"Willie!" I said. "Well, leastwise he's alive. I guess I better go see the sheriff."

"But what about those men who shot Uncle Frank? Won't they be looking for you?" she protested.

"I'll be careful, Miss," I said.

"Please," she said, "call me Annabelle. I feel like we're old friends, Mister . . .?"

"You can call me Del," I said. "Del Tackett."

"My goodness," she said. "Did you know that Uncle Frank's friend is named Tackett, too?"

"Yes, ma'am. I knowed your uncle had a friend named Tackett. That's why I come up this way. I wished to see if we was kin."

"Well, didn't you see him yesterday at the restaurant?"

"That was Tackett?" I fairly shouted it.

"Why yes. Uncle Frank calls him BeeBee."

I sat there silent, stunned. Then the thoughts began racing through my head. BeeBee Tackett. Ben Bill Tackett. Bennett William Tackett. My God! My God! Could BeeBee Tackett be my father? If he was why didn't he come back to Ma—to Ma and me—after the war?

No wonder he kind of looked familiar. I was looking at an older, greyer, certainly better-looking version of me. Not quite so big, but big enough. And ramrod straight like a soldier. Ben Bill Tackett. Damn—I caught myself—dang!

"Mr. Tackett—Del—are you all right?" It was Annabelle calling me back to reality. "Are you all right?" she repeated. "You looked kind of funny."

I shook my head to clear it. "Yes, 'm. I'm fine. But now I got things I got to do. I got to find out about Willie and then I got to find out about Mr. Tackett."

Her face fell. "I was hop—." Then with a struggle she smiled. "Of course. Go, but please be careful. And remember, you're always welcome here."

I looked at her hard and I could see she was putting on a brave front. "You was hopin'?"

"Nothing. Nothing at all." She shook her head.

"Annabelle," I said. "If you and me are gonna be friends you got to level with me."

"I was hoping," she said slowly, "that you would stay here until Doctor Marien gets back. He said he knew a woman in town who might help me take care of Uncle Frank. He said if she would come he'd bring her over. I just don't know if I can care for Uncle Frank all by myself."

My heart sank. I really wanted to go hunting Willie. And after that, BeeBee Tackett.

"I'll stay for a bit," I said. "If ya got that soup ready, let's see if we can get some down him."

Frank Honerock was lying in his bed with his head propped up on a couple of down pillows. His eyes were closed and his cheeks were pale, but he seemed to be breathing regular and there was some color in his lips.

"Uncle Frank," Annabelle said softly, and again, "Uncle Frank."

Honerock slowly opened his eyes. "Is that you, Mother?" he whispered. "It hurts, Mother. It hurts."

"It's me, Uncle Frank. Annabelle."

"Oh, it's you, Annabelle," he whispered slowly. "What are you doing in here?"

"You were shot, Uncle Frank. Mr. Tackett carried you home." With an effort Honerock focused his eyes on me. "You're not Tackett."

"Yes, sir," I said. "I'm Del Tackett. I ain't that other Tackett." Annabelle interrupted. "We can talk later, Uncle Frank. I've brought you some soup. Mr. Tackett—Del, could you lift up his head a little?"

I did what she asked and she slow and careful spooned him several mouthfuls of soup. After the fourth or fifth one he shook his head, "No more."

I laid his head back on his pillow and he drifted off. Annabelle tucked the covers around him and we headed back to the kitchen. I brought her a bucket of water in from the backyard well, then watched whilst she cleaned up the dishes. She no sooner finished than there was a heavy knock on the front door. I followed Annabelle when she went to answer it, keeping my hand close to my gun butt. I wasn't taking no chances.

The man at the door was Doctor Marien, and he'd brought with him a dishwater blonde in her middle thirties. She had a careworn face, already beginning to be lined, and blue eyes that were older than she was by maybe a hundred years. She wore a plain grey dress and a wide-brimmed grey hat. She looked familiar, but I couldn't place her.

"Miss Annabelle," Marien said. "This is Miss Mayer. Lisa Mayer. She has agreed to come stay with you as long as you need her. I have told her you will pay her two dollars a day. Miss Mayer and I have worked together before. She is very familiar with gunshot wounds."

"Yes, yes, of course," Annabelle replied. "Miss Mayer, I'm awfully glad to see you. Won't you please come in?"

"I'll let you two get acquainted," Marien said. "I'll be going now, but I'll be back to change the dressings on his wounds this afternoon."

"Doc," I interrupted, "ya seen any strangers wanderin' around the town this mornin'?"

He shook his head. "Town looks quiet today," he said. "We had a little ruckus yesterday afternoon in the cafe before Mr. Honerock was shot." He looked at me closer. "Come to think of it, you may have been involved." I shrugged and he went on talking. "Doesn't make any difference. The kid who started it got knocked around a bit before the sheriff could get control of things. He's got him in jail now, mainly for safe-keeping, I hear."

"That's Willie, my saddle pard," I said. "He was tryin' to get me out of a jam. I hope he ain't bad hurt."

"He was bloodied up a bit, but nothing serious."

"Well, I guess I'd better go bail him out."

I said my goodbyes to the two women and told Annabelle I'd stop in before I left town.

"I was hoping you would stay here," she said.

"You'll be all right," I told her. "Them Websterbys seem to of left town. Besides, it's me they're after, not yer uncle."

"Whoever it is they're after, they're terrible people. Please, please be careful."

She reached up, put her hands behind my head, pulled my mouth down to hers, and kissed me a goodbye kiss, but one that held the promise of more to come if I wished it.

I undid her hands and put them down by her sides, with the guilty thought of Esme running through my mind.

"I'll drop by afore I leave town and check in on yer uncle," I said.

"Doc, if it's all right with you I'll walk back to town with ya."

"Glad of your company," Marien said. He turned to Lisa Mayer and patted her on the shoulder. "You take good care of Mr. Honerock. This town needs him,"

"I will," she said softly. "You know I will."

"That Annabelle's a nice girl," I said to Marien as we walked away.

"She seems to have taken a shine to you," he replied.

"I got me a girl down Arizona way," I said.

He laughed. "Arizona's a long way from here." Then he got serious. "I hope Lisa Mayer works out."

"Why wouldn't she?" I asked.

"She's good," he said. "She's very good. Especially with bullet wounds. I've used her before in another town. But she's not a nurse by profession."

"Don't think that matters if she's good," I said.

"You don't understand," he said. "She has another profession."

"What do ya mean?" I asked.

"Don't say anything to Miss Owensmith," he admonished. "But Lisa is one of the girls on the line. She's been working the cow towns and mining towns for the last fifteen years. The men who know her call her 'Moaning Lisa.'"

"Heard of her," I said noncommittally, knowing now why she looked familiar.

He went on, "If a nice girl like Miss Owensmith finds out about her, she might ask her to leave even though she needs her."

"I won't say nothin' if you won't," I said.

"That's a deal. I just hope nobody else who knows her finds out what she's doing and talks."

"If she's as good as you say, why don't ya hire her as yer nurse?" I asked.

He gave a sardonic chuckle. "My real occupation gets in the way of that."

"Yer real occupation?" I asked.

"Drinking," he said as we arrived at the main street. "Sheriff's office is down that way."

He left me and walked off in the other direction, toward the Grand Saloon.

CHAPTER 12

WHEN I WALKED into the sheriff's office, he was sitting behind his desk cleaning his fingernails with a folding Barlow pocket knife like the one I carried. His fingers were like the rest of him—short and thick. It seemed to me as if every time I walked into a sheriff's office the sheriff or his deputy was sitting there cleaning his fingernails. No doubt about it, law enforcement in the western lands was a dirty job.

Without looking up, the sheriff asked, "What kin I do for ya?"

"I understand you got my saddle pardner locked up. Young feller name of Willie."

He looked up then. "Oh, it's you. Thought ya was long gone."

"I will be as soon as ya turn Willie loose."

"I ain't so sure," he said. "Sheriff from down Kolakoka way says yer a escaped prisoner. Asked me to hold ya if ya came in. Says yer pard, that Willie kid, helped ya escape. Wants us to hold him, too."

"Ya can't do that, Sheriff," I told him. "Ya turn me and Willie over to von Cart and old man Websterby and they'll lynch us soon as they get us out of town."

"Maybe, maybe not," he said. "But if he's the sheriff down there I got to turn ya over to him. He said he'd check in with me this afternoon."

He stood up. "Now gimme yer gun, Mister."

He reached out his hand, clean fingernails and all, so as I could hand it to him, but I didn't. Instead I taken it out of its holster and pointed it at him.

"Don't be a fool, Tackett. Drop it," he growled.

"Don't you be a fool and try to take it from me because if I have to, I'll kill ya," I said, keeping my voice low and conversational, but putting a mean tone into it.

He moved as if to go around his desk, but I cocked the hammer on the six-shooter and he stopped in his tracks. "I said, 'Don't be a fool, Tackett.' "

"I ain't bein' a fool, Sheriff. I'm just tryin' to stay alive. Now, I tell ya what. First you take your gun out and lay it gentle-like on the floor. Then ya reach up on that wall there and grab that set of keys. Then ya walk around that desk real slow, keepin' yer hands where I can see 'em. And then we'll go back and let ya trade places with Willie."

He started to argue but I gestured at him with the gun and said, "Move!"

He reached down careful and took out his gun and set it on the floor. Then he straightened up and took the keys off the hook and came around the desk. Then, with no warning at all, he flang the keys at me and lunged for me, trying in one motion to brush my gun aside and grab me in a bear hug. But I was watching for him to try something dumb and I ducked the keys, stepped inside his outstretched arms and clouted him alongside the head with the barrel of the six-shooter. The blow didn't knock him out but it dropped him to his knees and from there he fell forward onto his hands.

Whilst he was shaking his head to clear away the cobwebs, I leaned over and pick up the keys which had hit the wall and then fallen on to the floor.

"I didn't wanta do that, Sheriff," I said. "And I don't wanta have to do it again. Now get up and do what yer told and we won't have no more trouble. Move, now, 'cause time's a-wastin'."

He staggered to his feet, leaned against the wall a moment, then turned and headed for the door leading to the cells. There was two of them, it turned out.

Willie was in the left one, lying on the bunk. He stood up when we came in and I could see they'd worked him over pretty good. His lips were swollen and cut and one eye was closed and black and there was blood on the front of his shirt, either from his nose or his mouth. But he had a cocky look on his pimply face and he grinned a lopsided grin at me. " 'Bout time," he said.

"Looks like they give ya a beatin', kid."

He nodded. "I didn't see one of 'em and he coldcocked me while I was firin' them shots over their heads. Just tryin' to scare 'em is all. I dropped my gun when he hit me and then they beat the hell out of me. If it hadn't been for the sheriff here they'd of prolly kilt me.

"What'd ya have to go and beat him up for?"

"I'll tell ya later, kid," I said. "Right now, we gotta get goin' before von Cart and them Websterbys come back. Now open up that cell, Sheriff," I ordered, handing him the keys.

In few seconds Willie was out and the sheriff was in.

"You be still for a little while, Sheriff," I said. "I don't wanta have to tie and gag ya."

He glared at me, for which I didn't blame him, but he didn't say anything. He was still pretty woozy and there was a bump growing alongside his head where I'd hit him. Whilst I watched, he staggered over to the bunk and lay down with his face to the wall, bump side of his head up.

Willie followed me back into the office and whilst I was hanging the keys back on their hook he took down his gunbelt which was hung on a nail in the wall. "I lost my gun in the fight," he admitted, sounding shamed.

I went over and picked up the sheriff's gun and handed it to him. "This'll hold ya," I said. "Let's get goin'. Where are the horses?"

"At the stable," he said, opening the door. But he hadn't even set a foot outside when he ducked back inside. "Damn!" he swore. "Websterby and his bunch are comin' up the road."

I went to the window and looked. There was half a dozen horsemen riding down the street from the north with Tod Websterby in front and Sheriff Curt von Cart at his side. Since there wasn't no place to stay in town, I figured they'd camped up the road a ways and now were coming back to see if I was still around.

I watched von Cart rein his horse over to the hitchrack in front of the sheriff's office whilst the other five went by a little ways and pulled up at the Grand Saloon on the other side of the street. Von Cart dismounted, tied his horse to the hitchrack, and stomped up to the door. When he came in I was sitting at the sheriff's desk.

"Howdy, Sheriff," I said. "What can we do for ya today?"

He couldn't of looked more surprised if he'd found a polecat in his saddlebag.

"What have ya done with the sheriff?" he demanded, and his hand started drifting toward his gun.

"Don't try it," I said. "Willie there has his gun pointed right at the back of yer head. Show him, Willie."

Willie, who'd been standing on the far side of the door, stepped over and pressed the muzzle of the sheriff's old Colt .45 against the back of von Cart's neck. Von Cart's face went white and his eyes got big.

"He ain't gonna shoot ya," I said. "Not if ya do what yer told.

"Willie, get his gun. Then let's find some rope and we'll take him back with the other sheriff and tie 'em both up. We'd best gag 'em, too. Don't want 'em raisin' a ruckus."

We put von Cart in the other cell and bound and gagged him.

The other sheriff—I still didn't know his name and Willie wasn't no help in the matter—was snoring away on his bunk. I figured I must have hurt him more than I thought. Or maybe his head was softer than it was supposed to be.

But dang! I hadn't wanted to hurt the man. I had nothing against him, and Ma had brought me up to respect the law. Which I did, as a rule, although I always figured that the men the people hired to enforce the law ought to respect it, too. If they didn't, why should the rest of us?

"We'll leave him be," I told Willie. "He'll prob'ly sleep the rest of the day. Besides, he ain't in no shape to cause trouble."

We went back to the office and I peeked out the window again. The street was empty except for a few horses and one buggy tied to hitchingracks. The stable was at the north end of town, in the other direction from the Grand Saloon.

I handed Willie a silver dollar. "You go first," I said, "and get the horses saddled. Soon as I think yer ready, I'll come on down. If ya hear any shootin' up this way you'll know something's wrong, so take off. No sense in both of us gettin' kilt or captured."

"Thanks," Willie said. "But if there's shootin', why I guess I'll just come a-runnin'. Wouldn't wanta miss a good fight."

He went out the door and strolled nonchalantly down the street looking like he didn't have a care in the world. Watching him go I felt good. He'd growed up a lot in just a few days and he'd gone from trying to prove how brave he was by gunfightin' me to being my friend. No, not my friend, but my saddle pardner. Almost over night he'd gone from being a wild-eyed kid to someone I could depend on. He was going to be a good man. In some ways he already was.

I gave him five minutes and was just about to leave when the door opened and a cowboy I recognized as one of Websterby's men came in.

"Seen the sher ..." he started, then recognized me and stopped mid-word. A second look and he saw my gun pointed right at him. "Don't shoot," he said, putting up his hands.

"Wasn't plannin' on it," I said. "What do ya want, anyway?"

"Websterby sent me to see what was takin' von Cart so long. Said to tell him to hurry it up."

"Well, dang," I said. "I'll take ya in to where you can tell him. Course it looks like I'm gonna have to ask ya to stay with him a while. Drop yer gunbelt, then take off yer belt."

He was a redhead with a red face that began to get redder still from anger and from being made to look like a dang fool.

"What ya gonna do?" he asked, unbuckling his gunbelt.

"Gonna tie ya up is all. Now take off yer belt."

He taken it off and his jeans began to fall down. He dropped his hands to grab at them, but not before I saw he wasn't wearing no underwear.

"Well I'll be danged," I chuckled. "Ma always told me that, man or boy, a feller oughta wear underwear. Even when we didn't have no money, she always scraped up enough for a pair of long johns."

His face went from red to white he was so mad and he taken a step toward me, but he stopped when I waved my gun at him. Besides, he couldn't have done nothing anyway what with having to hold his pants up. I turned him around and marched him back to the cell where von Cart was tied. In a minute I had him tied with his belt and gagged with his own dirty handkerchief.

"So long, fellers," I said with a grin. "Someone'll come by after a while and let ya out—if yer lucky. And by the way, Red, don't try standin' up 'til someone unties yer hands."

Feeling pretty good about things, I left, locking the cell behind me and stuffing the keys in my pocket. No sense, I figured, in making it easy for whoever found them to turn them loose.

Aside from two or three townsfolk, the street was empty as I walked down to the livery stable. Willie had the horse we'd borrowed from the old man—maybe my old man, I thought—and Old Dobbin saddled and was getting nervous when I showed up.

"Was beginnin' to worry," he said.

"Had a visitor. 'Nother one of Websterby's men. I put him in with von Cart," I said, mounting up.

"Where we headin'?" he asked.

"I wanta go find that old man who brang us to town yesterday."

"What about Botrish and Clara?" he asked. "They ride into town when Websterby's here and they might not get out."

"Yer right," I said. "We got to find them first. Then we'll go hunt up that old man."

"What do ya want him for?" Willie asked. "Ya hardly know him."

"Dang it, Willie," I said. "He just may be my Pa. Besides that ya borrowed his horse. Remember?

"But after I talk to him, Willie, one way or another—if we're kin or if we're not—I'm goin' back to Arizona. It taken this trip for me to realize that Esme and Beauty mean more to me than anything in the world, includin' any kinfolk I might have. But you 'n' me is saddle pardners, Willie. So if ya want, you can come with me to the R-Bar-R and be a part of our family."

"I'd like to ride along," he said, acting real casual but I saw him using a finger to wipe away a tear when he thought I wasn't looking.

"Ya never told me yer last name, Willie."

"Brown," he said. "William Brown, but Maw always called me Willie."

We'd been riding south for about three hours and it was mid-afternoon when Willie pointed ahead and off to the right to a line of trees.

"Smoke," he said.

I looked where he pointed.

"Might be them," I said. "Or it might not. Spread out and we'll ease up there and take a look."

We'd almost got up to the trees when a man stepped out from behind one of them.

"Tackett," he said. "Thought sure you'd be in Cutbank by now." He laughed and added, "Lookin' up a preacher for the weddin'."

"Coe," I said. "Good to see ya. Ya got Botrish and Clara with ya?"

He nodded.

"What about them injuns?"

"Injuns are notional," he said. "You know that. They decided they didn't want to go to the white man's village. And they didn't make any fuss when we said we was goin' anyway. So here we are. We figured to camp here for the night so's we could ride into Cutbank in the daylight. How come you ain't there?"

"You got coffee?" I asked.

"Yep."

"Fine. Let's go get some and I'll tell ya what's been happenin'."

CHAPTER 13

THEY WERE CAMPED amongst the trees next to a creek, right where it curved south to run on a line with the mountains on the west of it. Zell Botrish was sitting with his back to a tree and looked like he had dozed off.

Clara jumped to her feet when she saw us, a warm welcoming smile on her round face. "I thought you were going to wait for us in Cutbank."

"Been a change in plans." I said shortly. "I think you best douse that fire. You can see the smoke a mile away."

"Ain't no injuns around this neck of the woods," Zell Botrish said from where he sat.

"I ain't worried about injuns," I told him. "I'm worried about Tod Websterby. Him and his men like as not are on our trail and I and Willie left tracks that ain't gonna be hard to foller."

"How many men with him?" he asked.

"Hard to tell. He come into town with five, mebbe six, but I s'pect he's got that many more. And it may be that sheriff up there has put together a posse to tag along."

Zell looked around. "We can fight 'em off if there ain't too many of 'em. There's five of us and Clara. And she can handle a gun as good as most men."

"I ain't lookin' for a fight," I said. "I didn't come up here lookin' for no war. I want to get done what I come here to do and get back down to Arizona afore the snow flies."

"I ain't runnin'," Willie said, glaring at me.

"Looky here, Willie," I said, glaring right back at him. "There are times to fight and times to run. Right now is the time to avoid a fight if there's any way we can."

"I ain't runnin," he repeated stubbornly.

"We run now and they'll chase us to hell and gone," Coe said.

I shrugged. "You all can stay here and fight if you want," I said. "Me, I'm headin' for the hills. Willie, I think this is the crick we went up when Websterby was chasin' us the other day. If I'm right, old BeeBee Tackett's ranch ain't far from here and I got to see him. You-uns can come along if ya wanta. Or you can stay and wait for Websterby. It's up to you."

"Bad mens come," Chief Whitewater said.

The big Indian walked silently into the clearing, appearing, it seemed like, from out of nowhere. He had this strange habit of disappearing without notice and returning the same way. Anyhow, I was glad to see him. He was carrying his bayonet and a rifle and leading a tall red appaloosa gelding that looked like it could go all day, even with Whitewater on its back.

"Where in tarnation did you come from?" I asked, feeling both startled and pleased at the same time.

He waved a hand toward Cutbank.

"I look for you," he said. "You come from Cutbank. I wait and see who follow. Then I come."

"How many are comin?"

He spread the fingers of one hand three times.

"Fifteen more or less," I said. "That sheriff done put together a posse. In a hurry, too. How much time we got afore they get here?"

"Pretty soon now," he said.

"Coe, you and Willie wanta stay and fight 'em?" I asked.

Coe shook his head. "I'll trail along with you."

I looked around at the rest of them. "Comin' or stayin'?"

"We ain't total damn fools. We're comin'," Botrish said.

"Me, too," Willie said.

"Ya know this country, Chief?" I asked.

"Me know."

"Ya know BeeBee Tackett?"

He nodded again. "Me know."

"You know where his ranch is at?"

"Me know."

"The injun seems to know everything," Coe muttered.

Whitewater looked at him and I thought I saw just the trace of a smile. "Me know," he said.

"Can ya take us there?"

He nodded one more time. "We go," he said, putting a foot in a stirrup and swinging aboard the appaloosa.

He led the way, splashing across the creek and turning downstream. After a little ways he turned back into the stream 'til he came to a rocky stretch. He turned the appaloosa toward the mountains and it scrambled out onto the rocks with the rest of us following.

I pulled Old Dobbin alongside him. "Which way's the ranch?" I asked. He pointed west and a little north where I could see the outlines of a plateau poking out from the mountains. "There," he said. "We go in my way."

"How long?" I asked.

"Two, maybe three hours."

I looked at the lowering sun. "Be dark by then. Maybe we better camp and go in in the mornin'."

He shook his head. "Moon tonight. Plenty light. We go in."

"Whatever you say," I said.

I turned back to the others. "Chief says it's a two- or three-hour ride. Says there's a moon tonight, though, and that we oughta go until we get there. Ya make it, Zell?"

Botrish's arm was still in a sling on account of the wound he'd got in the fight with Bailey Harbor and his men and he looked a little pale.

"Don't worry about me, Tackett," he said. "I'll make it."

Whitewater led the way through the sparse woods and around rocks and large boulders, always heading toward the rim of the plateau, just where it stuck out from the mountain. We climbed slow but steady, and as the sun began to sink, a chill wind started blowing down from the north.

Riding alongside of me Coe leaned over and said, "Don't look like yer gonna make it."

"What does that mean?" I asked.

"Like as not that wind'll bring an early snow. Take a look. There's clouds headed this way."

"Dang!" I swore. I trotted Old Dobbin up to Whitewater.

"Coe thinks it's gonna snow, Chief. Can we get there quicker?"

Whitewater shook his head. "No snow tonight. Tomorrow, maybe." Nevertheless he kicked the appaloosa in the flanks and the spotted red horse moved out at a faster pace.

Whitewater was right. A bright moon lighted the landscape after the sun went down, shining through a hazy layer of clouds. The way grew steeper the nearer we got to the base of the mesa, but suddenly Whitewater located a narrow, seldom used trail that he must of been looking for. It zig-zagged back and forth, but it led us steadily upward, and we moved along steadily 'til the trail took a sharp turn and we found ourselves riding on the flat land of the mesa itself.

"Not far now," Whitewater said, urging his horse into a trot.

Less than five minutes later, we cantered into the yard of BeeBee Tackett's ranch, but the house wasn't there any more. The chimney still stood, along with the rock walls of the older part of the house and some charred timbers, but that was all. The barn had been burned down, too.

"Dang, dang, dang," I swore, dismounting and walking over to take a closer look. What the old man feared had happened. Websterby had burned him out.

We made a quick search but found no sign of a body, which I really didn't expect to find seeing as how I figured Websterby had burned him out whilst he was riding to town with Willie and me.

"Looks to me like the old man got away," I said to no one in particular. "If he didn't, we'll find him in the morning. Best thing for us to do is camp here tonight. It don't seem likely that posse'll be trailin' us in the dark. Best we don't light a fire, though."

Standing there in the moonlight, looking at the ruins of the ranchhouse, I wondered what BeeBee Tackett would do. But I didn't wonder long. I knew what I would do if it had been me Websterby burned out. I would go after him. I would hunt him down and get my pound of flesh if it taken me the rest of my life.

And that old man just maybe was my father. At the very least he was a Tackett, which meant we had the same blood. So yes, I knew what he would do. He would do the same as I would do. He would find Tod Websterby if he had to hunt him to hell and back and when he found him he would make him pay.

Willie and Coe walked up to look at the ruins.

"What do ya suppose happened to that old man?" Willie asked.

"If that old man is who I think he is ain't nothin' happened to him," I said. "If that old man is who I think he is, Tod Websterby better hunt hisself a hole because that old man is goin' after him."

"Ya talkin' about the owner of this here place?" Coe asked.

"Uh huh," I grunted.

"Ya know him?"

"Some."

"Well, who is he anyway?"

I turned and looked at him. "Guy, if I'm right, that old man is my Pa. And I got to go find him and help him. You-uns can do what ya want but I'm ridin' to Cutbank."

I turned and headed for Old Dobbin.

Coe grabbed my arm. "Hold up, Tackett. The horses are beat and so are we. If yer smart you'll grab a couple hours rest. Then I'll go with ya."

"Me, too," Willie said.

"Clara and me 'll trail along, too," Botrish said. "Fact is, we'll be safer from that posse in town that we are here. Leastwise I can find a place for Clara. Maybe old man Honerock will take her in."

I didn't say anything. It didn't seem to make much sense telling him Honerock might be dead by now. I took my hand off the saddle horn.

"Yer right," I told Coe. "We'll rest a mite, then I'm goin' in. But this is my fight. You can ride to town with me if ya want but when we get there ya best stay outa the way.

"Chief?" I said, looking around, but the big Indian had disappeared.

I unsaddled Old Dobbin and rubbed him down with a couple of handfuls of dried grass and picketed him where he could graze a bit. Then I unrolled my blankets under a nearby tree and lay down, using my saddle as a pillow. I was just drifting off to sleep when I felt someone close by and looked up. It was Clara and she was spreading her blankets beside me.

"You oughtn't to do that," I protested. "It ain't proper."

"You've been ignoring me all day and I want to be near you," she said.

"Clara," I said. "I done told ya. I got a girl waitin' for me down Arizona way."

"She's there and I'm here," she said

"And so is yer old man," I said, turning away from her. "Now go away and let me sleep."

The next thing I knowed she'd leaned over and kissed me on the cheek.

"I'll make you love me. You'll see," she whispered and walked away into the darkness, carrying her blankets with her.

Dang, I thought, and double dang! Why couldn't she pick on Coe or some injun like Whitewater? I surely didn't need the trouble a pretty girl could bring, especially out on the trail. And she was a pretty girl, no two ways about it. I could see her in my mind's eye as she walked away. Pretty face, big black eyes, white teeth, nice smile, good figure.

Dang! I danged again. I'd better be careful. I'd slipped once, back there in Abilene with a lonesome schoolteacher named Ada Venn. I still felt guilty about that and I sure enough didn't want to slip again. Not that I'd been no puritan during my years on the trail, but now there was a woman down in Arizona that I truly loved. And in my heart I knew she was the only woman I had ever loved or would ever love, and I was determined to stay true to her.

Thinking good thoughts I drifted off to sleep.

The moon was still high when I woke up. Except for some gentle snoring, the rest of the camp was still. I sat up and pulled on my boots. I rolled up my blankets, picked them up in one hand and my saddle in the other, and cat-footed over to Old Dobbin. When I had him saddled I led him around the edge of the camp and down between the remains of the house and the barn where I picked up the trail that BeeBee Tackett had taken us on to Cutbank.

This was one time I didn't want no help. I thought I knew where the old man who might be my Pa would hole up 'til he could figure out a way to get at Tod Websterby. And a man alone would have a lot less chance of being spotted sneaking into Cutbank than two or three. Of course, if I was seen I'd be in big trouble, but that would be so even if Willie and Coe come along. No sense in getting them killed because of me.

I climbed aboard Old Dobbin and he picked his way slow and careful down the trail. Once or twice I thought I heard something in back of me and off to one side and each time I stopped to listen. Then, hearing nothing more, I rode on, figuring it was some animal out there, or maybe a rock falling.

The moon was down but the eastern sky was beginning to lighten when I rode into the back yard of Frank Honerock's house. There was a stable more like a small barn behind the house and I figured it would have three or four stalls in it.

Dismounting, I led Old Dobbin over to the barn and carefully opened the door. It didn't squeak, for which I blessed Honerock. Leading Old Dobbin inside I closed the door behind us. It was pitch dark and I fumbled a farmer match out of my vest pocket, struck it on the side of my jeans, and held it high so as to get a quick look-see at the layout of the barn.

When the match flared, something hard jabbed me in the back and a low voice carrying just the hint of a southern drawl said, "Move and you're dead."

"I ain't movin'," I said.

I felt the pressure on my back ease up some and then the voice said, "Do I know you?"

"You Tackett?" I asked.

"I am," he said. "And you?"

"Tackett, too," I said. "Del Tackett. And yer BeeBee Tackett."

The pressure eased more. "You're a Tackett?" There was astonishment in his voice.

"Yep."

The pressure increased on my back at the same time I felt him lifting my six-shooter from its holster, and a second later I heard my gun land on the dirt floor several feet away. "Now, Mr. Tackett, if that's who you are, get out another match and light it, then turn around so I can see you, but be very careful because this old six-shooter has a hair trigger and if it went off there wouldn't be very much left of you."

"Mr. Tackett, I come here lookin' fer you," I told him. "And I ain't about to do anything dumb, at least not 'til we've had a chance to talk."

Then I did what he told me to do. I got out a match and, not wishing to make any sudden movements, scratched it with my thumbnail. Holding it just above my face I turned around slow.

"All right," he said. "I know you. Put out the match and we'll go into the house and talk."

Well, that's what I'd come all this way for.

"Fair enough," I said, and blew out the match.

CHAPTER 14

I ASKED BEEBEE Tackett to open the barn door a mite and by the dim early morning light that filtered in I unsaddled Old Dobbin and put him in an empty stall. I grabbed a handful of hay and gave him a quick rubdown, then forked in some more hay for him to chew on, and followed BeeBee up to the house.

BeeBee Tackett. That's how I thought of him then, not knowing if he was my Pa or even if we were kin. But I hoped I was soon to find out.

Lamplight shone through the kitchen window, and when BeeBee knocked on the back door Annabelle opened it.

"Please come in, Mr. Tackett." Then she saw me and her eyes widened. "Both Mr. Tacketts, won't you please come in?" she invited.

We tromped in and sat down at the big kitchen table and she promptly filled two mugs with steaming hot black coffee. It was black and strong and it tasted good.

"How's yer uncle, Miss Annabelle?" I asked.

"He's conscious and he's taking soup and other liquids. I think he even has a little color in his cheeks. Miss Mayer is taking good care of him. She'll be joining us in a minute."

"That was Websterby's men who shot him?" BeeBee said. It was a statement and a question both.

"They thought he was me," I said. "But when they seen he wasn't, they didn't care."

"Websterby wouldn't have cared if it had been the angel Gabriel he shot," BeeBee said. There was something close to hatred in his voice.

"I guess you know him from somewheres," I said.

119

"For a long time. I knew him during the war," he said, adding almost as an afterthought, "and I learned to hate him. I never knew he was in Montana, or anywhere else as far as that goes, until the other day or I'd have tracked him down before. He's given me new reason to do so now."

He didn't say anything more and we both went silent. I had a thousand questions to ask him, but I wanted to be alone with him when I asked them. Annabelle brought over the pot and refilled our mugs and just about then Lisa Mayer walked in. She looked tired and I guessed she'd been sitting up most of the night with Honerock.

She went over to the stove and poured herself a mugful of coffee.

"Your uncle's askin' fer you," she told Annabelle.

Annabelle hurried out and Lisa Mayer came over and sat at the end of the table, looking first at BeeBee and then at me.

"Knew there was two Tacketts out here somewhere," she said. "But I never 'spected to see 'em both in the same room."

"Hello, Lisa," BeeBee said. "I never expected to see you in Frank Honerock's house."

"I'm his nurse," she said. "And I'm a damn good nurse and I don't expect neither of you to talk about nothing else. Miss Annabelle's a nice lady and she don't need to know nothin' 'cept that I'm takin' care of her uncle."

"Mornin', Moanin'," I grinned. "Thought I recognized you the other day."

"Don't you call me that," she snapped. She stopped talking and all of a sudden a tear rolled down her cheek. "It wouldn't hurt ya none to give a girl a chance."

I felt bad right off. "I'm sorry, Lisa," I said. "I ain't gonna say nothin', and old BeeBee here ain't about to neither."

"Not a word, Lisa," BeeBee promised, and reached over and patted her hand.

She wiped the tear away with a hanky she fished from her bosom and finished her coffee without saying another word. Then she got up and went over to the stove where a kettle of water was heating.

"I gotta take care of my patient," she said, picking up the kettle and walking out of the room.

"Neither one of us was very nice to her," BeeBee said after she was gone.

"That's a woman with a good heart," I said. "And we kind of shamed ourselves." Then I grinned at him. "Must run in the family."

"What do you mean by that?"

I looked him right in the eye. "I think yer my Pa."

"And I think you're General Grant," he said.

I quit smiling. "I wasn't funnin' ya, BeeBee."

"If you weren't," he said, "I think you had better explain yourself."

"Mr. Tackett—BeeBee, I come all the way from Arizona lookin' for you without even knowin' if we was kin. I've gone all my life thinkin' I had no kin except for Ma, and she died a while back, and then I hear about you and I come here to see if we was kinfolk. Ya got to help me." I knew I looked and sounded desperate. "I got to know."

"Calm down, boy," he said. "Frank Honerock told me about you a while back. He said the daughter of an old friend of his was thinking of marrying a man named Tackett and he asked me if we were related. I told him I thought I still had relatives in Virginia but none that I knew of out in the West. And I thought that ended that. So I'm surprised to see you."

"Was you ever married, BeeBee?" I asked.

A look of sadness crossed his face. "Once. Briefly. But I had to leave her when the war came along and when I finally got back she had disappeared and nobody knew where she had gone.

"Ya have any children?"

"I heard we had a baby boy but I went off to war right before he was born and I don't know whether he lived or not. It's possible, but I don't know. I only got one letter all during the war and that was shortly after I left. I searched for my wife for a while after the war, but her parents were dead and there wasn't any kind of a clue to what happened to her. After a while I gave up and came West."

"They call ya BeeBee. Is yer real name Bennett William Tackett?"

He stared at me. "How would you know that?"

"I told ya you're my Pa. His name was Bennett William Tackett but Ma called him Ben Bill and I figure that was where the BeeBee come from."

Now it was his turn to ask questions. "Where are you from, boy?"

"The high mountains of California."

"You born there?"

"Ma took me there when I was little. Afore that we was in Carson City. We come West from Philadelphia when I was hardly more'n a baby."

"Who is 'we'? Was your mother married? Did she have a husband?"

"I don't know all that much," I said. "Ma never talked much about our life afore we come to Lodestone. Lodestone, that's a minin' town up in the high sierras on the California side. But she was never married that I remember.

"Most of what I know I found out readin' a diary Ma left behind when she died. And there wasn't all that much in it. Never knowed her first name until I read the diary. But she never mentioned no man exceptin' you."

"Geraldine Carmen Groupe," he said so soft I hardly could hear. "Gerry."

He looked over at me. "You're William Delligan Tackett?"

I nodded, not being able to speak, I was so choked up. We got up almost together and in a second I was hugging him and saying, "Pa," over and over and he was hugging me and saying, "My son. My son."

In a minute we stood back and looked at each other and there was tears running down both our faces. I got my handkerchief out of my hip pocket and blowed my nose. My Pa did the same.

"We've got a lot to talk about, son," he said.

But it was not to be right then. There was a heavy knock on the back door and Pa went to answer it whilst I ducked out of the kitchen and into the darkness of the hallway. And danged if it wasn't the sheriff.

"Good morning, Sheriff Alecks," BeeBee Tackett said in his soft drawl. "What brings you here this morning?"

"I might ask ya the same thing," the sheriff said.

"I came here to visit my friend, Frank Honerock. He was shot the other night and is in serious condition. Or hadn't you heard?" There was more than a speck of sarcasm in Pa's voice.

But the sheriff missed it. "I heard," he said. "Come by to see if he was well enough to talk to."

"I heard you and Tod Websterby were out with a posse," Pa said.

"Been tryin' to run down that other feller who says his name is Tackett. He's wanted down Kolakoka way. When I went to arrest him he coldcocked me and took off. Him and that saddle pard of his. That Willie kid. Took a posse after 'em all right, but lost 'em. And I got too much to do to keep huntin' 'em. That Kolokoka sheriff von Cart and the rancher who come with him, Websterby—I guess you know him—are stayin' on their trail. 'Sides, I got me a hunch them two might head back this way. I'll tell ya one thing. If I get my hands on that other Tackett, he'll wish I hadn't."

The sheriff touched his head gently where I'd slugged him. "Say, BeeBee, I smell coffee. Kin ya spare a cup?"

Pa stepped aside and the sheriff stomped in and sat down at the table. Pa found a clean mug in the kitchen cupboard, filled it with coffee, and handed it to Alecks.

"Maybe you could find the time to look for whoever it was who shot Frank," he said.

"I got to talk to Frank first."

"Frank's talked a little bit," Pa said. "He thinks Websterby or his men did it. He thinks they mistook him for the man who calls himself Tackett. They were after him, you know. They talked about lynching him. It was Tackett, by the way, who found Frank and carried him home."

The sheriff took a swallow of coffee. "How do ya know it wasn't him who shot Frank?"

Pa shook his head. "It wouldn't make much sense, would it, for Tackett to shoot Frank and then carry him home? Besides, he hardly knew him."

"Yer right, but it don't make no difference. I find him, I'm gonna arrest him for assaultin' a officer of the law."

I ducked back away from the doorway where I'd been standing, watching and listening to the two of them, tiptoed into the parlor and sat down on the couch. Dang! Here I was in trouble with two sheriffs, and me a man whose Ma had always taught him to respect the law. Well, dang, I wouldn't of slugged him if he hadn't rushed me that way.

I moved back up to the doorway so's I could listen some more.

"Wouldn't it be better to try to find the man or men who shot Frank?" I heard Pa ask gently.

The sheriff's rough voice carried easily into the parlor. "No way to find 'em now 'less someone saw it happen or someone confesses, and that ain't likely. I was just scoutin' around some this mornin'," Alecks said. "Seen the light and the smoke from the chimney. Thought maybe I could beg a cup of coffee. Ya think I could see Frank?"

"He's a sick man, Sheriff. Unless Doc Marien says different it would probably be best to wait a day or two."

Steps echoed down the hallway as they talked and a figure passed by the parlor door. Then I heard Annabelle's voice and there was no warmth in it.

"Sheriff Alecks, what brings you here so early?"

"The smell and taste of yer good coffee, Miss Annabelle," Alecks said, and danged if he hadn't oiled all the roughness out his voice. And it hit me. Somewhere along the line the sheriff had decided to make a play for the lady and it didn't sound like it was something she welcomed.

"Someone shot Uncle Frank," she said coldly. "Isn't it time you arrested that someone?"

"I was just tellin' BeeBee, and I want ya to know I'm gonna do everything I can to catch the fella who done it."

"You might start with Mr. Websterby," she said. "Uncle Frank thinks it was him."

"I'll be needin' to talk to yer uncle, Miss Annabelle."

"You'll have to talk to Dr. Marien about that," she said. "At present he says Uncle Frank can't see anyone."

I heard a chair scrape and the sheriff said, "I'll talk to Marien and when he says it's all right I'll drop back. Be seein' ya, BeeBee. You, too, Miss Annabelle."

A moment later I heard the back door slam.

I got up and went into the kitchen as Annabelle was saying, "I can't stand that man, even if he is the sheriff. He asked Uncle Frank if he could call on me and Uncle Frank said no. He's nice enough and he means well but he's old enough to be my father."

BeeBee smiled at her through his beard. "It's not age that matters, Miss Annabelle. It's breeding. But I think your uncle was right. He's not your kind."

Just then Lisa Mayer came into the kitchen. "I heard that," she said. "I'd marry him in a minute if he'd have me."

"You're too good for him, Lisa," Pa said.

She laughed bitterly. "Thanks, Mr. Tackett," she said. "Yer too kind."

Annabelle looked at her. "Oh, Lisa, Mr. Tackett is right. You are too good for him. But just you wait. The right man will come along for you one day. For me, too, I hope."

That kind of talk always makes me uncomfortable, so I quick changed the subject.

"Miss Annabelle," I said, "me and BeeBee here got some private talkin' to do. Be all right with you if we used the parlor?"

She looked at me warmly, too warmly, I thought. "Of course, Mr. Tackett. Please be my guest. I imagine it isn't often two members of your family get together."

"That's mighty kind of you, Miss Annabelle," I said. I picked up my coffee mug, filled it and BeeBee's, and we stepped into the parlor.

I sat on the couch and he sat across from me in a big old leather-covered chair that Frank Honerock had worn shiny.

"You go first," I said. "I got to know all about us. Then I'll tell ya my side of the story."

CHAPTER 15

P<small>A LOOKED AT</small> me from across the room.

"Maybe I had better start from the beginning. The Tacketts are an old Southern family. Tacketts have been in America more than two hundred years. Before the war many of them were large land owners and, wrong as it may seem today, slave owners.

"Tacketts fought in the Revolution against the British and again in the War of 1812 against the British."

"Pa," I interrupted, "I'm ashamed to say it but I'm a ignorant man. I never had no schoolin'. I never learnt to read and write 'til I was growed. Nobody ever taught me or learnt me anything about this country. There wasn't no school where I growed up and Ma was too busy just keepin' body and soul together to teach me.

"All I know is that you left Ma and me and went off to fight for the South in the War Between the States and I ain't even sure I know what it was fought about. Slavery, some folks say, but it's beyond me why any man would want to own another man or why any man would let hisself be owned. Anyways, whatever the reason was, it must of been important to you because you was gone a long time and you never come back."

"I came back, son, as soon as I could," Pa said soberly. "But I'd been captured and was a prisoner of war and the Yankees kept me in prison for more than a year after the war ended.

"Some prisoners were exchanged early but they kept me and made me pay every day for nearly three years. Slave labor like few black men ever faced. Half rations. All because I helped my general and six other officers escape from that hell hole. Son, after those others escaped, the Yankees put me in a hole that wasn't big enough to lie down in and kept me there a month. What food I had they dropped down to me and they hauled my slop out in a bucket and they didn't much give a damn if they spilled it or not. There was mildew—green mildew—on me when I got out and I stunk enough to make a man vomit.

"Hate was the only thing that kept me from going crazy. Hate for the man who put me in that hole and kept me there."

He quit talking for a moment and stared off into space. "Strange, isn't it, Del, that the man who put me there and made my life a living hell for nearly three years is the same man who's been hunting you? Major Tod Websterby." He spit the name out and the hate in his voice came through loud and clear.

He went on: "When they finally freed me I was nothing but skin and bones. They turned me loose without a penny and only the clothes on my back and a tattered Confederate flag that I'd managed to keep hidden from them. The clothes I was wearing were the same Confederate uniform I was captured in, hardly the thing a man would choose to wear in the heart of Yankee country. My prison was in Columbus, Ohio. My wife, the last time I saw her, was more than five hundred miles away in Philadelphia.

"I started walking east. The first day I stopped at three different farm houses to offer to work for food. At each one they saw my uniform and drove me off. At one farm they set the dogs on me. I beat them off with a stick, but not before one tore my trousers and slashed my leg.

"That night I found a ramshackle barn and sneaked in and spent the night in a pile of hay. I'd gone without food all day and was totally exhausted. In the morning I was awakened by someone kicking me in the ribs and cursing me.

"It was the farmer who owned the place, a big, burly man who needed a shave and some clean overalls. He hauled me to my feet by the front of my uniform coat and knocked me down with a smashing blow to my face. As I told you, son, I was exhausted and weak, looking more like a scarecrow than a man.

"When I was down he kicked me again and again until I thought my ribs were broken. Then he told me I had better 'get the hell out of here because if you're not gone when I get back I'll kill you, you dirty rebel bastard.'

"As he turned away I staggered to my feet and saw a pitchfork leaning against the wall. In blind anger I grabbed it and with all my strength drove it into his back. One of the tines must have hit his heart because he gave a kind of gurgling noise, took a step or two, and went down flat on his face, and never moved or made a sound after that.

"After I made certain he was dead I searched him and found a clasp knife in his pocket. It was all he was carrying. I took it and I still carry it. Looking around the barn I found a heavy metal rod and, carrying it as a weapon, I walked up to the back door and went in without knocking.

"There was a woman standing at the stove. I have never forgotten her. She had long black hair and when she turned around I saw that she was young, probably in her early twenties. She had a tired, worried face, gaunt to the point of emaciation, and was nearly as thin as I was. Her plain cotton dress hung loosely on her the way my clothes hung on me.

" 'Good morning, ma'am,' I said. 'Your husband sent me. He said it would be all right if you were to give me some breakfast.'

"She laughed and it wasn't a pleasant laugh. 'You're lying,' she said. 'If my husband knew you were here he'd beat you within an inch of your life and run you off or kill you, which ever suited his fancy. And if he finds me talking to you he'll beat me within an inch of my life, also. So please go away. Now.'

" 'Your husband beats you, ma'am?' I said.

" 'Please go, before he comes in. He'll be here any minute.'

" 'He's not coming,' I told her. 'And he won't ever beat you again.'

"I saw her black eyes widen. 'You killed him.'

" 'I had to, ma'am. I'm sorry, but I had to. He would have beaten me to death if I hadn't.'

"Her face froze over for a minute, but she didn't cry.

" 'I'm glad,' she said unexpectedly. 'He was a mean, cruel, vicious man. I married him because I was all alone with no money and no place to go, and I tried to be a good wife to him. But nothing ever satisfied him. He beat me, sometimes every day. One of his beatings killed my baby before it was born. He didn't care.'

"She started to cry then and as I moved toward her she came into my arms and weak as I was I held her there and stroked her long black hair for what seemed like an hour. After a while she quit crying and stepped back and wiped her nose with a bit of a rag she pulled from her bosom. Then she bade me sit down at the kitchen table and she fed me the breakfast she had been preparing for her dead husband.

"While I ate she told me that they'd come from Pennsylvania but her husband had been preparing to move farther west because he wasn't making a go of it in Ohio.

" 'He was a lazy and ignorant man who hated the world because he was poor. He would never have made a go of it anywhere,' she said.

"He had sold what livestock they had except for the two horses that would pull the wagon. He had planned to load the wagon that day and they were to leave the following morning.

" 'I don't rightly know what to do now,' she said. 'I have kinfolk east of Pittsburgh and I could go there if I had enough money.'

" 'Lucy,' I said—she'd told me her name was Lucy Edding— 'Lucy, I'm heading for Philadelphia where I left a pregnant wife nearly six years ago. If I could rest up here for a few days I would be glad to help you load the wagon and drive you to Pittsburgh. It would be a favor to me since it is on the way to Philadelphia.'

" 'I'd be beholden to you,' she said.

"The barn had a dirt floor and with Lucy's help I managed to dig a shallow grave for her husband whose name was Adwin Edding. After we tamped the dirt down we piled hay on top of it. Lucy said they had never neighbored and she was sure that if any of their neighbors came by they would just think they had gone away.

"After we buried her husband she dressed the wound where the dog had bitten me and while I slept in their bed she searched the house and finally found where he had hidden a little stash of money, enough to see us through to Pittsburgh.

"I rested there for three days, eating the plain but hearty meals that Lucy cooked. She was a good cook and she set out to fatten up the both of us. At night I slept in the same bed with her but I never touched her until the third night and then, when I reached for her, she came to me. Son, I had been without a woman for nearly six years and, well, she was there and I was there and we both had needs."

I didn't say nothing, remembering as I did that night with a school-teacher named Ada Venn. You don't mean for some things to happen, but they happen anyway. And I had no trouble understanding what it was with Pa and Lucy Edding—not love, but loneliness and need.

Pa said that was the only night he ever touched her. The next day he loaded her few possessions into the wagon, hitched up the two horses, and headed out for Pittsburgh. He had found some old clothes of Edding's that he'd outgrown and, while they didn't fit Pa very well, they were better than a Confederate uniform there in Ohio and Pennsylvania.

Pa was lucky in one way. Edding owned an old army Colt .44 and a Sharps carbine rifle that he must of brought home from the war. Lucy said he'd never talked much about the war but she thought he had fought with the Union forces for about a year and then deserted. One thing about it: Edding was a slovenly farmer, but he kept his guns oiled and in first rate condition, and he kept a large store of ammunition on hand.

The wagon trip to Pittsburgh was uneventful and they found an uncle of hers in Wasco, the small town east of Pittsburgh that she had mentioned. He ran a general store there and Pa hired on as a handy man for a month to earn enough money to go on to Philadelphia by train. He never told them he was a graduate of West Point or that he'd been a major in General Morgan's Confederate army that had advanced farther north than any other rebel force. Even with Lucy, all he told her was that he had been a Confederate officer.

Pa managed to take a train from Pittsburgh to Philadelphia but when he reached the Groupe house the new owners couldn't tell him anything. They had bought it from a family Pa never heard of and they, in turn, had never heard of the Groupes or of a young mother named Geraldine Groupe Tackett.

Pa spent six months taking odd jobs to sustain himself whilst he searched for Ma, but by this time she was long gone to the West, to Carson City and on to the little town of Lodestone in the high sierras of California where I grew up.

The few people he located who knew or had known of the Groupes knew only that Ma's parents were dead. They did not know what had happened to their daughter.

"It was as if she had disappeared into thin air," Pa said.

After six months Pa gave up the search and took a train to Washington. He bought a horse there and made his way to the site of the family home in southwestern Virginia. But it was gone, too. It had been sacked and burned by Union guerillas and his parents had been butchered. They were buried in unmarked graves and he couldn't even find those.

"I had one brother and he never came back from the war and nobody I talked to knew what had become of him. I knew I had other relatives throughout the South but they were all strangers to me. The fact was, son, everyone I had ever loved was gone. When I finally faced up to that fact I said, 'To hell with it, to hell with the East, to hell with the South, to hell with the whole damned country.'

"The horse I'd bought had gone lame so I stole a horse from a farm owned by Yankees who had driven off the rightful owners, and I headed south and west.

"I was a desperate and embittered man. I owned nothing except the clothes on my back, the pistol and rifle that I had taken from Ad Edding, and the Confederate flag that I still carried with me to remind me never to forget how the North had treated its prisoners of war and what it had done to my family.

"Winter was coming on so I took a route that led me down through the Tennessee mountains. From there I planned to ride south to Memphis and either cross the Mississippi there and go on into Arkansas, or else continue south to New Orleans.

"I was a lonesome man and a wandering man by then and it didn't seem to make much difference where I went. I just wanted to get far away from every place I knew and start life all over again.

"An early snowstorm hit as I was making my way through the Tennessee mountains. Fortunately for me, as night came on I spotted a cabin. A woman lived there with two young boys and she made me welcome. Funny thing, she had a name almost like ours—Sackett."

"Sackett!" I said. "Pa, there's Sacketts all over the West includin' a bunch of 'em down Mora way in southern Colorado. A whole clan of 'em. Gunfighters they are, or was. I've had to duck out of trouble more'n once 'cause someone thought I was a Sackett and wanted to try me with a gun."

"Probably the same family," Pa said. "I've run into one or two of them out here myself. The woman said she had sons out west and that she was hoping to join them as soon as they got settled. I don't know if she ever did."

"That's like 'em," I said. "Real clannish the whole bunch of 'em. Must be ten or fifteen, anyways. I run into some of 'em once. They'd got a bum steer. Someone told 'em there was a Sackett in trouble down Arizona way, in a town called Nora, and they come to help. When they found out it was a Tackett—me—and not a Sackett, they left. Didn't bother me none, though, because by then my troubles was behind me.

"But one of 'em stayed after the rest had went. Name of Hacken Sackett. Said he was a cousin of the rest of 'em but was from New Jersey, wherever that is. Said if I ever needed him to holler and he'd come. Couple of times I would of if I'd knowed where he was at. I think he thought his kin shouldn't of walked away like they did, even if I wasn't no Sackett.

"Anyhow, go on, Pa. This is right interestin'."

Pa settled back on the sofa, taken a pipe out from a pouch he had tied to his belt, put some tobacco in it, tamped it down and asked

133

if I had a match. I handed him a farmer match from my vest pocket. He lit the pipe, taken a couple of big puffs, and got ready to start talking again.

About then Annabelle came in with a couple of mugfuls of coffee and left without saying a word. Pa and me each taken a couple of sips. It was hot and black and it tasted good. Then he picked up where he'd left off when I interrupted.

"I stayed with them almost a week waiting for the storm to end and the snow to melt. I chopped some wood for her and made a few repairs around the place. The boys were willing but still too young to do all the work that needed doing.

"When I left she gave me a knife, the finest I've ever seen, that she said a Gypsy peddler had left for her husband a year or two before. Apparently he had saved the Gypsy's life at one time and the peddler was showing his gratitude. Unfortunately, she said, her husband had gone to the western mountains a number of years before and had never returned or even sent word, and she was certain he was dead."

Pa reached back and withdrew a knife from a sheath that hung between his shoulder blades and showed it to me. It surely was a fine knife, made of some sort of steel that never showed rust and it had some curious markings etched in its blade.

I laughed, pulled up my left pant leg, and taken from the case I wore on the inside of my leg the twin to Pa's knife. "I got it from a sailor down in San Pedro one time. He said he got it from a Gypsy sailor whose life he saved."

"It might have been the same man, Gypsies being the wanderers that they are," Pa said.

After the snow had melted some, Pa taken off and rode down out of the mountains and picked up the Natchez Trace that led to the Mississippi. Those were dangerous days in the wilderness and the backwoods, with men made homeless by the war still wandering the land. Many were thieves and robbers and murderers, and many a traveler heading for the river never made it.

But Pa rode careful-like, avoiding farms and country inns when he could and camping out nights off the beaten track. He had two or three narrow escapes but each time was able to get away with his horse and his hide. Eventually he made his way to Memphis where his southern drawl made him welcome amongst the townsfolk. He found a job clerking in a store, but one night in a saloon he got talked into joining a poker game. Pa had played some before and during the war and even in the Yankee prison, and he wasn't no greenhorn at it.

He won a considerable sum that night, more than he could make in six months clerking. The next day he quit his job and for the next few nights made the rounds of the saloons, watching the poker games, noticing what went on but not playing.

At one game he saw a man, obviously a professional gambler, win almost every hand. Suddenly one of the other players threw down his cards, accused the gambler of cheating, and threatened to kill him. The gambler calmly drew a pistol from under his coat and shot his accuser dead. Only the dead man had friends in the crowd and they began closing in on the gambler, and Pa could see the man was in serious trouble. Pa'd been watching that game carefully and was sure the gambler wasn't cheating, so he drew his own pistol and stepped to the gambler's side and the two of them, holding off the crowd with their pistols, backed out of the saloon, and got away in the dark.

The gambler was a man of about forty. He was tall and pale with almost white hair and brows and pale blue eyes. His name was Rick Mavver and he'd come down just that day on a steamer from St. Louis. He was headed for New Orleans where he lived and where he was part owner of a saloon and gambling hall.

"I'm going to sell out," he told Pa as they walked down a dark street to the pier where the steamer was docked. "I'm a gambler not a businessman."

"I've been looking for you," Pa told him.

Mavver stared at him. "I never saw you before in my life."

"Nevertheless, I've been looking for you," Pa said. He went on to explain how he'd won a lot of money in a poker game several nights before, but he realized that if he was to make a living gambling he'd have to be a lot more skillful at it than he was.

"I want you to teach me," he told Mavver.

"In that case you're going to have to help me get out of town," Mavver said. "That dead man back there has friends and they're bound to set the law on me. And if I'm arrested I'm sure to be tried and convicted—at least for manslaughter. After all I'm a stranger here."

The owner of the store where Pa had been working, a man named Lee Fraker, had rented Pa a room in back of the store but after Pa quit, Fraker told him he would have to be out of the room by the end of the month when his rent was up.

Pa took Mavver there and put him up for the night. The next day early he went down to the dock and, following Mavver's directions, found the gambler's stateroom, packed his things, and nonchalantly walked away right when a detail of Memphis police was boarding the steamer to search for Mavver.

Using money Mavver given him, Pa next went to the livery stable where he kept his own horse, and bought a nondescript roan gelding and a saddle. At dark Pa brought both horses around to the back of the store and the two men left the city at a gallop, heading south.

Traveling mostly at night along country roads away from the Mississippi and living largely off the land, they made their way to New Orleans. Every day on that ride, while they waited for dark to fall, Pa took lessons from Rick Mavver: How to shuffle cards to bring the right card to the top or to the bottom, how to deal the second or third card down from the top, how to mark a deck.

"You may never need any of this," Mavver told him, "but if you know how to do it, it'll be easier for you to spot someone who's trying to cheat you."

Pa showed me his fingers, long and slim and, despite his age, still dextrous.

"I had good hands, I was a quick learner and I spent long hours practicing," he said. "By the time I left New Orleans the following spring I was as good as Mavver was."

Mavver also taught him how to look for the little telltale signs of stress in a man who might be bluffing.

"A big part of being a really successful gambler is learning to read the men you're playing with. In many ways that is more important than learning to handle and read the cards," Mavver told him.

By the time summer came, Pa was a first-class professional gambler and had a goodly sum deposited in a major New Orleans bank. But he wasn't comfortable gambling for a living.

"I just didn't like the idea of living off other men's earnings," he said. "Somehow it didn't seem right. A friendly game is one thing. Taking advantage of other men's weaknesses is something else again."

At any rate Pa decided that it was time to drift, so he withdrew some of his money from the bank, bought himself a tall, strong gelding and a pinto pack horse and headed west. He asked Mavver if he wanted to go along but Mavver, who had not, after all, sold his share in the saloon, shook his head no.

"No matter where you go," he said when he and Pa were saying goodbye, "always remember—this is your base, your home. Whenever you're tired of wandering you can always come back here."

The two men shook hands and Pa mounted up and trotted off, heading for the western lands and the wide open spaces.

CHAPTER 16

Pa WAS ABOUT to tell the story of how he finally settled in Montana when there was another knock on the front door. This time it was Doc Marien. Annabelle let him in and he went right to Frank Honerock's bedroom.

His arrival put a temporary end to Pa's story-telling.

"I'll tell you the rest some other time, son," he said. "The main thing I want you to remember is that I searched every corner of Philadelphia looking for some trace of you and your mother and I finally had to conclude that you were not to be found. I didn't want to think that the two of you were dead but I was unable to come to any other conclusion, so completely had you disappeared.

"In my wanderings over the next few years I listened and looked for some sign of your mother but I never went as far west as the sierras and the only time I even heard of another Tackett was when Frank Honerock mentioned you."

Whilst we waited to hear what Doc Marien had to report on Honerock, I told Pa a little about the R-Bar-R ranch down in the Arizona Territory and the girl who was waiting for me there. At least I hoped she was. I told him I had learned to read for two reasons: so that Esme would be proud of me and so I could read Ma's diary.

And I told him that this was the second time I'd gone off and left Esme and I knew that one day she'd tire of my wandering and find a good, steady man to settle down with.

"I don't know if I could stand that," I said. "One thing for sure, if she's there when I get back I ain't never gonna leave her again."

Pa got a grave look on his face.

"Is she an educated woman, Del?"

I nodded. "Her Pa was a army officer and she went to some sort of finishing school, I think they call it, somewheres back east."

"Love is a wonderful thing," Pa said. "Especially at the beginning. But there are some things love has difficulty surviving and one of those is when the man and the woman come from two different classes. An educated man eventually tires of an ignorant and uneducated wife no matter how many other good qualities she may have. And the opposite is true also."

I felt my face begin to redden under my growth of whiskers. "What are ya drivin' at, Pa?"

"You've got a lot of work ahead of you if you want to marry that woman and have her be proud of you as the years wear on," he said. "Son, you said yourself you're an uneducated man. You have no schooling. You only recently learned to read. It's to your credit that you have learned, but now you have to put that learning to use. You have to begin to talk like an educated man. You have to begin to act like one. Out here on the frontier under the circumstances in which most of us live, a lot of things don't matter: how we talk, what kind of manners we have. Out here if a man will keep his word and stand by his friends and pay his debts nothing else matters much. But times are changing. Montana will soon be a state. The law and laws are quickly coming to all parts of the West. The West itself is filling up with men and women who aren't coming to tame the land but to live in and build a land that is quickly being tamed. Many of them are educated people, people with money and resources, people with ambition and know-how. The girl you want to be your wife sounds as if she is one of those people. And if you want her to continue to love you and respect you and be proud of you, you are going to have to learn to fit in with this new breed of westerners."

"What are ya drivin' at, Pa?" I repeated somewhat gruffly, thinking I knew just what it was he was driving at and not liking it even a little bit.

"This is making you angry," he said. "And I don't blame you. I don't expect anyone has ever talked this way to you before. But you're my son and I think I have both a right and a duty to be blunt with you. And if you get angry I'll be sorry, but I couldn't be a father to you when you were growing up so I'm going to try to be one now.

"It isn't enough to know how to read, Del. It isn't enough to be a good cowman, or a good friend, or a loving husband. It ought to be, but it isn't. The truth is, it isn't enough to walk the walk. In a civilized society you have to learn how to talk the talk as well. You have to learn how to speak correct English. People will think you are an educated man if you do. You have to learn table manners. You have to learn how to act in polite society, because your wife will want the two of you, at least occasionally, to mingle in polite society. And when you do she will want to be proud of you, and will have a right to want to be proud of you.

"From everything I've seen of you so far, you are an instinctive gentleman and that makes me very proud, but I want you to have the trappings of a gentleman also, and so will your wife."

"I ain't sure that's possible, Pa," I said, still a little resentful. "I been the way I am for a long time now. Maybe too long to change. If what ya say is true, maybe the best thing is for me not to go back to the R-Bar-R at all. If Esme can't be proud of me, then she should find someone she can be proud of."

Pa smiled. "Think about it first, son. You don't seem to me to be the quitting kind."

We didn't talk for a minute or two, then I looked up at him. "I'll give it a try," I said. "Only you got to help."

"Gentlemen," a solemn voice said from the doorway. It was Doc Marien. Lisa Mayer was standing in back of him, an anguished look on her face. "I'd appreciate it if you gentlemen would join us," Marien said.

We followed him into the kitchen where Annabelle was busy making preparations for lunch. When she saw Marien's face her hand flew instinctively to her mouth and she murmured an anguished, "Oh, no."

Marien nodded his head. "I'm afraid so, Miss Annabelle. I had hoped he might make it and he seemed to rally there for a while, but he was too badly wounded and he had lost too much blood. I'm sorry. He was a good man."

She stood stock still for a moment, her eyes blank, then she started to crumble. I leaped and grabbed her before she could fall. Taking her in my arms, I carried her into the parlor and laid her down on the sofa. Lisa came in with a damp cloth and bathed her forehead and in a bit she opened her eyes and struggled to sit up.

"I fainted," she said, taking a sip of water from a glass Lisa handed her. "I'm sorry. But it was such a shock. Poor Uncle Frank. He was such a good man. And he was so good to—to me."

She tried to blink back her tears but it was no use and she started to cry softly. Lisa sat down beside her and hugged and comforted her as she wept.

After a while Annabelle took a handkerchief from her bosom and wiped her eyes. "Doctor Marien, can you arrange for the funeral?" she asked.

He nodded. "Tomorrow be all right?"

"Whatever you think is best," she said faintly.

"I'll take care of the details," he said. "Would you like Lisa to stay with you tonight?"

"I'd be grateful," she said.

I looked at Pa and he looked at me. His face was grim. "We had best be going, Miss Annabelle," he said. "We'll be attending the funeral. In the meantime you have troubles enough of your own without us bringing any of ours down on you."

We stood up and Pa went over and patted Annabelle on the shoulder. "We won't be going far. If you need anything tell the doctor. We'll stay in touch with him."

We headed for the kitchen door and Pa stepped out first and looked around.

"All clear," he said and we hurried to the barn and quickly saddled the horses. Again, before we led the horses from the barn, he stepped outside and taken a quick look around.

"Let's go," he said, and we mounted up and taken off at a fast trot toward the trees and brush that lined a small creek a quarter of a mile away. Once out of sight of the town, Pa pulled up and dismounted and I did the same. Leading our horses we splashed across the little creek and wound our way through the sparse growth toward the hills that lay beyond. Pa seemed to know where he was going so I followed along without asking no questions.

As we started to climb, Pa found what seemed to be a deer trail and we followed it a ways until it began to run alongside a large rocky outcropping. Pa slowed down then and appeared to be looking for something. When he found it he stopped. It was a two-foot-wide crack in the rock that seemed to lead nowhere. But Pa turned into it, leading his horse over gravelly ground in which we left no tracks.

The trail slanted upward and after a hundred yards or so it widened out into a small meadow at the end of a box canyon. It was grassy except for a thick clump of trees over against the eastern wall. It being late in the year, the grass was dry except around a spot where water seeped from the rock into a small pool. I could see where campfires had been built near it in the past, but not recently.

"I've been here before," Pa said. "I've ridden all the hills and mountains around this part of the country ever since I came into it more than ten years ago. There are signs that Indians used to camp here, but not since I've been coming here."

We dismounted and I looked around. The rocky walls of the canyon were steep for a horse but there were places where a man wouldn't have no trouble climbing out. I looked to where Pa was leading his horse and for the first time noticed that there was a sort of cave over to one side of the pool. It was more like a hollowed out place in the rock than a real cave, but it would give us some protection from the weather.

I was turning to inspect the rest of the canyon when I caught movement out of the corner of my eye. Without thinking, I hit the ground rolling, at the same time hollering, "Pa, watch out!"

I rolled behind a small clump of brush and waited for gunshots but all was quiet. I looked to where Pa had been but he had disappeared into the dark shadows of the cave. As I started to peer around the clump of brush I heard a voice call, "Ho, Tackett. I Chief Whitewater. I your friend."

Sure enough, there he was, walking across the meadow, carrying his army bayonet in one hand and leading his horse with the other.

I stood up feeling kind of sheepish. "You done scared the living wits out me, Chief," I said. "What're you doin' here, anyways?"

Moving up beside me Pa said, "Howdy, Chief. I didn't know you knew about this place."

"This Indian country. Whitewater know Indian country. Whitewater stay here many times."

"I see you two know each other," I said.

Pa nodded. "We've run into each other now and then."

"What you do here?" Whitewater asked.

"It's a good place to hole up for a while," Pa said. "It's close to town and Del and I have to go back there tomorrow."

"Afore we do that, Pa, I got to get word to Willie and Zell and them. They're up at what's left of your house."

Pa looked at me blankly.

"They burned ya out," I said.

Pa sighed. "I might have known.There's not one ounce of decency or kindness in Websterby. Not one ounce." He thought for a minute. Then he said, "Look. There's a back way out of here and from here it's an easy ride to the ranch. The chief can take you there if he will and you can bring them back here. This is a safer place than the ranch. I'll remain here on watch.

He smiled grimly. "Except for the chief, of course."

Without any more talk I mounted Old Dobbin and followed the chief back through the trees and into an opening in the canyon wall that the trees had hidden. We came up to Pa's ranch the back way, the way we taken to go to Cutbank.

When we were still several hundred yards away we heard a shot. Then a lot more shots. I started to touch my spurs to Old Dobbin, but thought better of it and reined up alongside Chief Whitewater who also had stopped.

"Looks like Websterby has maybe found our friends," I said. "We better ease up there and see if they need help."

He grunted his agreement and we dismounted and tied our horses to nearby trees. I taken a minute to dig out my moccasins to wear in place of my boots. Then we headed at a trot for the trail that led to where Pa's barn stood before Websterby burned it. I was carrying my Winchester rifle and had stuffed two extra boxes of shells into my jeans pockets.

When we came to the trail we moved along it without a sound until suddenly a woman's voice said, "Damn you two for sneaking up that way! I almost shot you."

It was Clara Botrish and she stepped out from behind a large sycamore tree holding a rifle and glaring at us.

"What's the shootin'?" I asked.

"Some of Websterby's men tried to come up the front way," she said. "Coe shot one of them. Then three of them tried coming over the rim of the mesa but they ducked back in a hurry when we blazed away at them. Then I came back here in case anyone tried sneaking in the back way."

"How many are there?" I asked.

"We don't know for sure," she said, "but there must be five or six, not counting the man Guy shot."

"Everybody here all right? Your pa and Willie and Coe?"

She nodded and I said, "Let's go see 'em. We got to get out of here pretty quick. They find this back way and they'll pin us down 'til were out of food and bullets both, Worse, come dark they can come right up through that notch and in the mornin' we'll be sittin' ducks. What do ya think, Chief?"

But Whitewater had disappeared again.

"Dang that injun!" I said, disgusted. "If he ain't gonna hang around I sure wish just for once he'd say where he's goin'."

Clara grinned at me. "Injuns are notional," she said.

"Seems to me you said that about white men a while back," I said.

"Them, too," she said.

I trotted back and got Old Dobbin, noticing that Whitewater had taken his horse when he left. Then me and Clara made our way up to the remains of the ranchhouse and I signaled the three men to gather around.

"Time we was gettin' out of here," I said. "We'll be sittin' ducks after dark. Willie, you pack up first, then whilst the others are gettin' their gear together you can keep watch. Every now and then fire yer rifle so they know we're still here. Me, I'm gonna grab a mite of shuteye. You-uns wake me up when yer ready to go."

I sat down with my back against a tree and dozed off. It didn't seem like more than a minute before Clara shook me awake. "Look," she exclaimed, pointing to the rim of the mesa.

A widening band of smoke was puffing up from below.

"Well I am danged," I said. Then I hollered, "Grab yer guns, fellers. They'll be comin' our way any minute." We were too far away to hear the crackle of the flames but I knew from the direction of the breeze that the fire would top out at the rim of the mesa, trapping Websterbys's men between it and our guns.

Sure enough, the first one came scrambling through the notch, carrying his rifle in both hands. I put a shot at his feet and he threw down the rifle and threw up his hands, hollering, "Don't shoot! Don't shoot!"

Behind him came six saddled horses frantically fighting their way onto the mesa, whinnying and blowing as they came, reins flying loose, one of them with a body draped crosswise on its saddle. Once on the mesa, the horses headed for us at a dead run and we scattered out to let them through, all the time keeping our eyes and rifles trained on the notch.

And through it, one at a time, came four more panicky men, tossing down their guns as they came and hoisting their hands in the air. We went out to meet them, keeping our guns at the ready. By this time we could see the flames shooting above the rim of the mesa and licking at the grass along its edges. Fortunately Pa's cattle had grazed the grass on the mesa short and what fire came over the rim burned itself out in a hurry.

I recognized two of the men. One had been with Bailey Harbor the day they tried to hang me and the other was Sheriff von Cart, who seemed to show up everywhere I was. I had mixed feelings about him. He'd stopped Bailey Harbor from lynching me, but then he'd disappeared when the mob back in Kolakoka was ready to storm the jail he'd locked me up in.

Then he showed up in Cutbank, riding with Tod Websterby—who was Harbor's boss—and tried to arrest me again.

It appeared to me that he was a weak man and an ambitious man, but not really a bad one. And I couldn't get over the feeling that I still owed him for stopping Bailey Harbor from hanging me.

"Coe," I said, "you and Willie keep an eye on these fellers. Von Cart, you come with me."

We walked a little ways away until we were out of earshot of the rest of them.

"Sheriff," I said. "What in tarnation ya got against me?"

He looked down at the ground. "Nothin'," he said. "But Websterby runs the country around Kolakoka and everybody pretty much does what he says."

"I thought you was gonna run for the legislature when Montana becomes a state."

"I meant to. But Websterby'll have the final say who the candidate is from our part of the country. You know how it is."

"It ain't gonna be you?"

He looked up at me. "That's for sure, now."

"I guess maybe I oughta hang ya with them other fellers," I said.

"I kept 'em from hangin' you once," he reminded me.

"If I was to turn ya loose what would ya do?" I asked.

"Head for Canada," he said. "It's not far and there's a lot of country up there."

"If I find ya back in the States I'll kill ya," I said.

"You won't," he promised.

"Go catch yer horse and high-tail it outa here," I said.

"Thanks," he said, and turned and headed for the band of horses, which had stopped running and begun to graze.

The fire was burning itself out along the edge of the mesa and the white smoke which had been thick for a few minutes was thinning fast. For a minute I wondered how the fire had started but then I knew. And I knew, too, where Chief Whitewater had gone.

I walked back to where the others were standing guard over Websterby's men.

"What'd ya do with von Cart?" Botrish asked.

"I owed him one so I turned him loose," I said. "He ain't comin' back."

"Yer prob'ly right," Botrish said. "He ain't no hero."

"What are we gonna do with these fellers?" he asked, gesturing at the four remaining Websterby men.

Willie butted in. "Hang 'em, I say."

"Willie!" Clara said sharply.

"Aw, I was just funnin'." he mumbled.

"All right, fellers," I said. "Unbuckle yer gunbelts and step back. Now empty yer pockets. Coe you check 'em to see they ain't got no hideout weapons."

When he'd done that I said, "All of ya take off yer belts. Now!"

There was some grumbling but they did it.

"Now all of ya take off yer boots and toss 'em over here."

There was more grumbling, but by the time Clara and Willie were back with their horses there was a pile of boots in front of me.

Paying no mind to their grousing, I stuffed the boots and guns willy-nilly into their saddlebags.

"We'll be leavin' you fellers here," I told them. "You can make yer way back to town, but if I was you I wouldn't be in no hurry."

One man began protesting. "You can't do this. It ain't right."

"If you want we'll take yer pants, too," I said.

Clara giggled, and the man quit talking.

Mounting our own horses and leading theirs we headed out the back way.

"Where are we going," Clara asked.

"Pa's got hisself a little hideout not too far from here," I told her. "We're headin' there."

"Pa?" she asked.

"Yup," I said. "The old feller what owns this place turns out to be my Pa. I been lookin' for him."

She didn't say nothing and we rode on in silence.

There was a horseman waiting at the spot where we were to pick up the dim trail back to where Pa was waiting. It was Chief White-water. He looked at me slyly as he reined his horse alongside of Old Dobbin.

"Big fire," he said. "Lightning, maybe."

CHAPTER 17

DARK WAS FALLING when our little troop wended its way into the box canyon. As we entered the trees I reined up.

"You-uns wait here," I said. "I'll go on in first and if everything's all right I'll holler. Chief, why don't ya come with me?"

We dismounted and began making our way through the narrow strip of woods. I was still wearing my moccasins and we moved silently to where we could see where Pa had pitched camp.

A bright fire was burning and I could see what looked like the shadow of a man against the canyon wall.

"Looks like everything's all right," I said and opened my mouth to call out. But I shut it without making a sound when Whitewater dug his fingers into my arm.

"Not good," he whispered. "Fire too bright."

I looked again. And as usual the chief was right. An old woodsman like Pa would of built a small sheltered fire that couldn't be seen from the top of the canyon and that could be kicked out in a hurry. This fire seemed meant to impress us that everything was all right.

"Looks like Pa might be in trouble," I said.

The chief grunted. "I go look."

Ghostlike, he slipped away into the darkness with me at his heels. The moon wasn't yet up and it was almost pitch black.

In the darkness outside the ring of firelight a horse whinnied. My heart sank. I knew one of our horses would whinny back and in a second one did.

Out of the darkness then—and not very far from Whitewater and me—a man said softly, "They're comin'."

A second voice admonished, "Keep still and let 'em come all the way in. Don't forget, the boss wants to hang that other Tackett feller, too."

Dang, I thought, old Tod Websterby still has a hate on for Pa just like Pa has for him. That might make some sense, but that mean old man came after me before he knew who I was. I'd come into the Montana Territory looking for kinfolk, not for trouble, but trouble was mostly what I'd found so far and it was him and his men who'd give it to me. And by now it didn't look as if I'd ever get out of it without facing him down, facing down a man I'd hardly met and didn't have a quarrel with, at least not until Bailey Harbor and his men started one.

Just then the chief touched my arm in a way that told me not to move. As he stole away I caught a glint of light reflected on his bayonet blade. In less than five minutes he was back and the bayonet was in its scabbard.

"One man dead," he muttered.

I shuddered in spite of myself. He'd moved and killed so quietly I hadn't heard a sound. I was real glad he was on my side.

"We wait now," he muttered again and the two of us hunkered down.

A voice between us and the fire said, "Where the hell do ya s'pose they are? They should of been here by now if they was comin'."

"Maybe it wasn't them. Maybe it was a wild horse or a stray," a second voice said.

"Likely," the first voice said. "Harris and Frank prob'ly have 'em penned up at the ranch. And even if they're comin' they'll prob'ly wait 'til mornin'. It's too damn dark to travel 'less ya know the way. Let's go ask that old man and see what he might know. A little more fire under his feet and he might be ready to talk."

My heart leaped up. At least Pa was alive. It sounded like they'd tortured him some, but still, he was alive.

Three shapes appeared by the fire, coming in from three different points in the meadow. The voice of the man who looked to be the leader said, "Where's Weenie Pete? Hey, Pete, come on in." He waited a few seconds, then said, "The sonofabitch must of fallen asleep. Newt, you go kick him awake. Tell him to get hisself in here."

One of the men moved out of the firelight and headed in our general direction. Out of the corner of my eye I saw Whitewater draw his bayonet.

Suddenly I heard a loud curse from the man called Newt and the sound of him running back to the fire.

"Pete's dead," he gasped. "Throat's been cut. Damn near took his head off. Look at all the damn blood on my hand."

"Hit the ground," their leader shouted. "Get out of the firelight."

In a second they had disappeared in the dark.

"What now?" I whispered to Whitewater.

"We wait," he whispered back.

We'd been waiting for less than a minute when the voice of the leader shouted, "You out there. Surrender or we'll kill this old man."

We continued to wait silently.

"Tackett! You hear me? We're gonna kill yer Paw."

Another minute and then an agonized scream came from the direction of the camp. I started to leap to my feet, then I sank back down. That wasn't Pa. Nothing they could do would make that old man scream.

"You hear that, Tackett?" the leader shouted. "That was yer Paw. You better surrender afore we kill him."

"Chief," I whispered. "If we don't surrender the only thing they can do is leave. They don't know who's out here or how many of us there are. But they do know the other way out. I'm gonna check on the others then I'll come back. In the meantime I think you oughta make sure they don't escape. That narrow opening there, one man could hold it against a hundred."

Without a word the chief started off toward the canyon opening whilst I eased away toward the trees. In a minute or two I was stumbling and fumbling my way through the pitch darkness of the grove. When I reached the place where I'd left the others, there was no one there.

"Dang," I swore softly.

Feeling around with my moccasined feet I found the thread of the trail we'd come in on and started to move down it. I thought for a second about the chief but realized he'd be better off by himself than with me, because for sure I wasn't no woodsman while he moved like the next thing to a ghost.

I've heard stories about men out here on the frontier who could track a snake across a flat rock, or spot an old Indian trail through the mountains that hadn't been walked on for a hundred years or tell one horse's hoof from another on hard ground or soft sand, or walk through a forest on a dark night and never step on a twig nor run into a tree. But none of them was me. Oh, I could track a little bit, and get along in the wilderness and live off the land if I had to. But basically I was just a big mountain boy who could handle a gun and a rope and a knife pretty well, even though I wasn't no Doc Holliday or Wes Hardin.

I could break a horse or handle the reins on a stagecoach or work in a mine. I'd rode shotgun, herded cows, been a deputy sheriff for a little while, panned gold and even owned a saloon. But if you wanted a real honest-to-goodness frontiersman or trapper or gunfighter or trail boss, then you'd better go get one of them Sacketts I was always being mistook for. Or that famous army scout folks called Hondo. Or maybe the feller who was prob'ly the best of them all, although he didn't have the reputation the others had because he'd always walked wide to avoid trouble if he could.

I'd run into him once on a ranch he owned down near the Four Corners country. His name was Lew Lamore and men who'd been in the West since it was young never made any bones about it—Lew Lamore was the best, or at least he was in his prime. He was the best with pistol or rifle or knife, the best with a rope, the best tracker and hunter, the best cattleman. He could speak the Indian sign language and was supposed to know seven different Indian languages. There wasn't a man he couldn't drink under the table and he had a way with cards that would put the slickest riverboat gambler to shame. And no man had ever beaten him in a rough-and-tumble fight.

Well, I wasn't him or even close and I wasn't none of them other fellers either. I was just big ol' Del Tackett from the high mountains of California, with more brawn than brains, making my way through life the best way I knew how. And now here I was, lost out in the middle of nowhere on a night so dark I couldn't see my hand in front of my face. My friends had disappeared and my horse along with them. My Pa had been captured by my enemies. Dang! What was a man to do?

I sat down and leaned back against a tree trying to puzzle things out. And it came to me. Zell and Clara and Guy Coe and Willie would have to fend for themselves for the time being. They weren't no tenderfeet. Zell and Guy had both been up the crick and over the mountain. They could take care of themselves. Me, I had to go back and try to rescue Pa. That was something I had to do.

I stood up, stretched and stood stark still with my hands in the air and the barrel of a gun poking me in the back.

"Don't move," a man's voice said.

I'd been holding my breath and now I exhaled, letting it all out of my lungs in one big sigh. "That you, Coe?" I asked.

"Tackett!" he said. "Thought it might be you but I wasn't takin' no chances. Where's the chief?"

"Guardin' the other entrance to the canyon. Four of Websterby's men are out there and they got Pa a prisoner. I got to try to turn him loose. I was just fixin' to go."

"Where's the others?"

"We moved back a ways to give us runnin' room if somethin' went wrong. We heard that scream and some shoutin' and I was just comin' up to take a look-see when I stumbled on you. Ya don't move real quiet, ya know."

"I never claimed to be no ghost," I said. "You better get back to the others. Me and Pa'll join ya if we can. If we don't make it, then you-uns had better head for Helena or some place where there's law."

"Who screamed?" he asked.

"Don't know. They tried to make us think it was Pa. But it weren't. The devil hisself couldn't make that old man holler."

"I'm goin' with ya," Coe said. "Ya might need some help."

"Better you stay with Clara and them. They'll need help if I don't get back. 'Sides we'd just get in each other's way."

I clapped him on the shoulder and moved off into the dark of the trees.

I followed the line of them to the wall of the canyon and begun to make my way along it to where the cave was. The fire was still burning but I figured that didn't mean Websterby's men were still there. If they were smart they'd be heading for the canyon entrance, unless of course they figured they'd run into a trap.

When I got close I dropped down on my hands and knees and crawled toward the fire. As I did so it came to me that I didn't hear any movement from the horses. In fact there wasn't no sound at all and no shadows that a man or a horse might make.

Of a sudden, down toward the canyon entrance I heard a loud cowboy yell, the rush of hoofs, and a bunch of shots.

Dang! Websterby's men had figured someone might be laying for them and decided their only chance was to bust out. Anyways, they were gone, or most of them were. There wasn't no way the chief could shoot them all.

I stood up and walked into the firelight. The camp was empty, but they'd been in such a hurry they'd left some of their gear behind, including a coffee pot and over against the wall of the cave a bedroll. Or was it? On second glance, it looked like a man asleep. Or dead. Pa?

I walked over and bent down to the figure. And danged if it wasn't Pa. He was bound and gagged and barefoot, but it was Pa.

I quick taken the gag out of his mouth. He worked his jaw a couple of times and said, "It took you long enough."

"You all right?" I asked, working to untie the knots that bound his hands.

In a moment I had him untied and he sat up and began rubbing his wrists.

"I'm fine except for a few blisters on my feet," he said. "I did a dumb thing is all. I dozed off and when I awoke they were here. I didn't have a chance."

"Why didn't they kill ya?"

"Some of them wanted to, but their leader said that Websterby wanted to hang you and me side by side. Also they had some idea that I knew where you were which is why they burned my feet, but they weren't really serious. They figured you'd be coming back, and, of course, you did."

"I come all right," I said. "But they done missed their chance to hang us."

"We won't give them another one," Pa said grimly.

"They taken off in a hurry," I said. "I guess they taken yer horses, too."

"Me get horse," Whitewater said, appearing from out of the dark. "One rider, three horses. Others run away."

I jumped. "Dang it, Chief," I said, "I wish you'd let me know when yer comin'. Yer allus scarin' the livin' daylights out of me."

"Rider bad hurt. You come," he said, ignoring my complaints.

"I'll wait here and hunt up my boots," Pa said. "They threw them out there somewhere."

"You walk all right," I asked.

"Sure, son. You go along with the chief. I'll be fine."

I followed Whitewater toward the canyon entrance. He led me to a lump on the ground that turned out to be a man I could barely see in the dark. He was sprawled on his back. I leaned over him and as I did his right arm came up and starlight reflected off the barrel of the six-shooter he was holding. As he fired, I threw myself to one side, clawing at my gun as I rolled away. There were no more shots and when I looked up I could see why.

Whitewater was pulling his bayonet out of the man's chest. He wiped it on the side of the feller's cowhide vest and stuck it back in its sheath.

"Him big fool," he said.

"Him big dead fool," I said, crawling to my feet. "Thanks, Chief. That's one more I owe ya."

"I get horses," he said and slipped away. I walked back to where Pa was waiting. He'd found his boots and was walking around kind of gingerly.

"Heard a shot," he said. "Are you all right?"

"Wounded man back there tried to shoot me," I explained. "The chief put him out of his misery with his bayonet."

"That's a wicked weapon," Pa said. "I've seen him use it before."

I was surprised. "You know him?"

"He's a Nez Perce," Pa said. "He had a falling out with Chief Joseph a number of years ago and came into this country. He has a cabin back in the mountains, but spends most of his time wandering these lands, hunting, fishing, enjoying the wilderness.

"Its a strange thing: he likes the white man. We came into this country about the same time and took a liking to each other. We've had long talks. He knows the white man will take over the land and he accepts that. He believes that when he dies the Indian's day will be gone. And he's probably right. That will be a shame, too. It seems to me that there is room in this land for the Indian and the white man to live side by side in peace, if only they will."

The clop of hoofs interrupted him and the chief walked into the firelight, leading three horses.

"We go now," he said.

Pa and me kicked out the fire, making sure it was cold and the three of us mounted up and headed toward the little patch of woods, back where our friends were waiting.

CHAPTER 18

Pa, WHO WAS as familiar with the land in that part of Montana as Chief Whitewater, took charge and headed us for the clump of trees that hid the other entrance to the box canyon. Coe was waiting for us at the edge of the woods.

As we rode I explained how the chief and I had found him, and in a few minutes we had joined up with Zell and Clara Botrish and Willie.

"Pa says he knows a good place to pitch camp," I told them. "Once we get settled in, we got to talk things over. Seems to me we been so busy runnin' we haven't had time to lay any plans. Come mornin' we oughta have some idea of what we're doin'."

Pa, who could see in the dark like an owl, led us back down the trail a little ways then veered off in the general direction of Cutbank which was about ten miles northeast of us.

We were in low hills now and the moon was up. Pa led us back into a little cove where some tall grass still grew even though there were dried cow chips lying around. The trickle of a stream flowed from the base of a rock at the steepest part of the hillside and there was a scattering of trees.

Pa reined up under a big sycamore. "We'll camp here," he said.

I felt sorry for him. He was old and tired and he'd had a rough day and his blistered feet had to be hurting something fierce. We all dismounted, Pa stepping down pretty tenderly.

"Can we have a fire?" Clara asked. "I'm cold and hungry."

"In the morning maybe," Pa replied. "We don't know who else is out here and a fire would be too easy to see. Come daylight we'll find a place to hide a small one and by then the chief will have scouted the area."

"Where is he?" Clara asked.

Pa chuckled. "Wherever he wants to be."

We unsaddled the horses, including the ones we taken from Websterby's men in that fight at the ranch. Using handfuls of dry grass, Willie and Coe and me rubbed them down. Pa taken his bed roll and I noticed he already had it opened up and was lying on it.

It gave me a guilty feeling. If I hadn't come along and messed up his life he'd be fine. He'd still have his ranch. And, oh yeah, old Frank Honerock would still be alive. All this trouble had come about because of me, because I thought I had a need to know if maybe I had kinfolk and wasn't all alone in this world. Dang! What was wrong with me? Finding out sure wasn't worth ruining some lives and losing some others.

Besides, when I came right down to it I wasn't alone even before I found Pa. I had the most wonderful girl in the world waiting for me in Arizona and good friends, too, like Lew Haight and Blackie Harrington down there on the R-Bar-R. Not to mention that big black dog named Beauty who, next to Esme Rankin, loved me best.

Well, I knew one thing for sure. Tomorrow I was going to start to put an end to all this nonsense. And as soon as I finished that job I was going home, back to the people I loved.

I shrugged and turned back to Willie and Guy Coe.

"We'll turn the extra horses loose in the mornin'," I said. "No sense in keepin' 'em with us. Someone catches us with 'em, they might try to hang us as horse thieves and I've done had enough of folks up here in Montana tryin' to hang me."

When we'd finished picketing the horses, I called everybody together around where Pa was laying.

"It looks to me," I said, "like I've brought a heap of trouble on everyone here even though that sure wasn't my intention. Old Todd Websterby thinks I'm a cow thief—which I ain't—and because of that him and his men are out huntin' down every one of us. If they catch us they'll hang us all 'ceptin' Clara, and I don't like to think what they'll do to her. "Anyways, I'm gettin' sick and tired of it. I wasn't huntin' trouble when I come to Montana and I been tryin' to avoid it ever since I got here but I'm changin' all of that beginnin' tomorrow. I know it ain't Christian but I got a lot of gettin' even to do. They've tried to lynch me twice. They burned down Pa's ranch and tortured him. They shot Zell here and mistreated Clara and they been chasin' us all over these hills.

"Well, I just want ya to know, startin' tomorrow it's my turn. Tomorrow, I quit runnin' and begin takin' it to 'em. But whilst I'm doin' that, I don't wanta have to worry about you-uns, which means I want ya to head out of here, all 'ceptin' Pa. He can hole up with Whitewater 'til his feet heal. The other four of ya oughta head for Helena or some other town where there's real law. Long as I keep Websterby and his gang busy here they won't have time to follow ya."

"I'm stayin'," Willie said. "You and me're saddle pards and I'm stayin'."

I couldn't see him in the dark but I could feel his pale blue eyes staring at me. "Suit yerself," I said.

"I think I'll stay, too," Coe drawled. "I ain't used to runnin', neither."

"We'll be goin'," Zell said softly. "Clara and me'll be headin' out in the mornin'."

"Father!" Clara said sharply.

"Don't argue, girl. We're goin'," Zell said and Clara, turning away, stayed silent. Zell turned to me. "I got my girl to look after, Del. Them is mean men out there and I wouldn't want nothin' happenin' to her. Not after what they put her through a couple of days back."

"You and Clara go on, Zell," I said. "That's what I want ya to do. We'll turn in now and you can leave at first light.

"Coe you take the first watch. Willie, you take the second and I'll take the third. We'll talk some more in the mornin'."

Pa spoke up then. "My feet are feeling better, but they're still pretty sore and I won't be getting much sleep. Why don't I take the first watch? I'll wake up Coe if I get sleepy."

Suddenly something occurred to me. "Coe, ya got any more of that salve ya used on Harbor?"

He chuckled at the memory. "Sure do."

He rummaged around in a saddlebag, dragged out a greasy tin, and handed it to Pa. "This'll ease the hurt," he said. "Help heal ya, too."

I reached over and took a dab of it and smelled it. It had a kind of tangy odor. "Smells like a ointment a sawbones I ran into down in Colorado uses," I said. "Where'd ya get it?"

"That's funny," Coe said. "I got it from a old injun down in that neck of the woods. He must of been a hundred years old. Said he come from a tribe I never heard of—the Mimbres or somethin' like that. I helped him through a winter down there a few years ago. He told me what plants to use. Said it was good for a lot of things. I could make a tea out of it and use it for a tonic or I could powder it and mix it with any kind of animal fat and use it as a healin' salve. It's great stuff for burns and cuts. I heard later that a drunk buffalo hunter shot the old man. Too bad."

He quit talking and I didn't say anything neither. I was remembering Ed Alliso, the barber-doctor-dentist down in Shalak Springs in southern Colorado where I'd owned a saloon for a little while. Alliso also used a lineament made from a recipe he'd gotten from an old Indian medicine man who later was shot by a drunken buffalo hunter. It had to have been the same man.

Strange, I thought, how people's paths cross. Even the big, wide-open West was a small world.

Pa finished rubbing the salve on his blistered feet. "Feels better already," he said. "You boys go on to sleep. I'll waken Willie after a bit."

It was well toward dawn before Coe wakened me.

"Thought you could use a little extra shuteye," he said. "And, by the way, Botrish and Clara taken off about a hour ago."

"They're good folk," I said. "If it hadn't of been for them ol' Bailey Harbor would of got me lynched back there in Kolakoka. I owe 'em."

"That Clara's quite a woman," he said—wistful, I thought.

"They'll be headin' for Helena," I said.

"We get this mess straightened out I might head that way myself," he said.

"You better take a bath first," I said. "She ain't about to take up with no smelly cowhand."

"Had me a bath just last month," he laughed, heading for his bedroll.

I let them sleep 'til the sun began turning a scattering of clouds in the east pink. I noticed with relief that the snow clouds seemed to have passed over. I wasn't anxious to get trapped out here in a snowstorm or to have winter come before I got back to the R-Bar-R.

With daylight Pa built a tiny fire under a spreading tree that filtered the smoke from the sticks of dry wood Willie and Coe had gathered. Pa's feet, thanks to Coe's lineament, were feeling a lot better and he moved around without hardly limping or wincing.

Whilst they were putting together some breakfast, I climbed to the top of the hill next to where we'd camped. I crawled the last few feet to the top and looked over. All I could see was a few stray cows and a small herd of buffalo off to the south. Lookin' north and east, all I could see of Cutbank was the haze from the smoke of the early morning cooking fires.

I went back down and picked up the tin cup of coffee Pa had poured for me. It was hot and it tasted good. So did the bacon and the frying-pan bread. Then I remembered I hadn't had nothing to eat since the morning before.

"I'm for ridin' right on into town," I said. "We can hole up in Honerock's barn and maybe we can send Annabelle on a stroll through town to see if there's any sign of Websterby and his men. Pa, ya know of any way we get there without bein' seen?"

"There's a stream north of here that runs in the back of Cutbank," Pa said. "It's a little out of the way but if we can get to it without being spotted, we can ride along the far side of it all the way to town. It's brush-lined all the way and there's not much chance of being seen."

We kicked out the fire, packed up, and saddled the horses, except for those we taken from Websterby's men. We turned them loose to run free or try to find their way home. Pa led the way, heading north and keeping the hills between us and Cutbank. When we reached the stream that flowed pretty much east and west, we splashed through it and headed east to Cutbank, still hidden from the town by trees and brush.

By late morning we'd begun to see a scattering of houses and cabins that told us we were nearing the town. It wasn't long afterward when Pa reined up. "We're pretty close to town now," he said, "and just a little way from Frank's place."

"Tell ya what," I said. "You-uns wait here and I'll go take a look and see if the coast is clear."

Before anyone could argue I touched my spurs lightly to Old Dobbin and we moved off through the trees, splashed across the stream, and spotted Honerock's house less than a quarter mile away.

It was quiet and peaceful without a soul moving about outside the house, although off to the right a little farther away I spotted a couple of horsemen riding down the main street of the town. A bird was singing somewhere and in the distance a dog barked.

Cantering up to the back of the house, I dismounted and tied Old Dobbin to a post and went up and knocked on the door. When it opened, danged if old Tod Websterby wasn't standing there with a Colt .45 six-shooter pointed right at my belly.

"Come right on in, Mr. Tackett." he grinned, showing yellow, tobacco-stained teeth. "We've been waitin' for you."

He stood aside and gestured me in with his gun. The first man I saw when I walked into the room was Sheriff von Cart.

"Thought you was headed for Canada," I said.

"Well, we all make mistakes," he said. "Soon as Montana becomes a state I'm runnin' for the legislature. Mr. Websterby and me have got it all fixed up."

"You talk too much, Von," Websterby growled.

Von Cart quit talking and dropped into one of the kitchen chairs. There were three other men sitting around the table, but I didn't know any of them.

"First thing you do is take your gun out of its holster very carefully and set it on the table," Websterby ordered. "You do it right and you may live a little longer."

Very carefully I took my six-shooter out of its holster and set it on the table.

"Whatever happened to ol' Bailey Harbor?" I asked.

"Be another week before he can sit in the saddle," Websterby said. "I've been thinkin' about takin' ya back there so's he can help hang ya. He'd be pretty unhappy if he was to miss that. First off, though, I want to catch old Ben Bill and maybe Botrish and his kid, if they're still around," Websterby said.

"I sure wouldn't want ol' Bailey to be unhappy," I said. "What ya got against old Ben Bill anyway?"

"He helped some men escape during the war and cost me my promotion," he said. "I wanted to hang him then but I was overruled. This time there's nobody here to overrule me.

"Say, boy. I hear tell you're his son. That so?"

"I think so," I said. "We ain't had time to compare a lot of notes, but it kinda looks like it."

"Well, we'll hang ya together, boy, and the two of ya can compare notes in hell."

Websterby grinned his wolfish grin again and come over close to me. He wasn't very big, about half a head shorter than me, but he was whipcord lean and bobcat mean.

Looking up at me he asked, "Where's the old man now?"

"Danged if I know," I said.

Without warning he backhanded me across the mouth. "I said, where's the old man?"

I wiped my mouth with the back of my forearm, adding a little blood to the dirt that already was heavy on the sleeve. Licking my lips, I said, "They taken off first thing this mornin', headin' for Helena. Botrish says there's a U.S. marshal there."

Without taking his eyes off of me, Websterby called, "Annen, you an' Nilwirth get over here and hold this tough guy while I beat some answers out of him."

"Dang it! I told ya the truth," I said.

Annen and Nilwirth could of been brothers. They were both big, hulking blond-headed brutes, neither one as tall as me but both a good deal heavier. Each one grabbed one of my arms and twisted it back into a hammer lock. And Websterby kneed me in the groin.

I would of doubled up from the awful aching pain but I couldn't because of the way Annen and Nilwirth were holding me. When I sagged it almost tore my arms out of their sockets.

I heard someone give out a agonized groan and it turned out to me.

"Where's the old man?" Websterby snarled.

"Helena," I groaned.

He hit me in the gut, putting all of his weight into the blow. I thought I was going to die. And I didn't care. I couldn't breathe. I couldn't fall down on the floor and curl up in a ball. I couldn't think.

Dimly I heard Websterby say, "Let him loose."

I fell to the floor and curled up in a ball. Someone kicked me in the back of the thigh but I hardly felt it.

In maybe five minutes Annen leaned over and yanked me into a sitting position. I could breathe but I was still in agony.

"Where's the old man?" Websterby demanded.

"Helena," I whispered.

"Get the girl," Websterby ordered.

Someone went to the parlor door and called, "Bring in the girl."

Then someone shoved Annabelle into the kitchen. She stumbled and would have fallen except that Annen caught her with one huge arm and dragged her to him. She fought to escape but he crushed her against his chest with one arm and with the other one brought her head to his so that they were lip to lip.

"Oww!" he yelled, shoving her away. "She bit me."

Annabelle stumbled backward and fell almost in my lap.

"I'll kill her," Annen snarled, spitting blood onto the kitchen floor.

"Later, Luke, later," Websterby said. "I have other uses for her now."

He turned to Nilwirth. "Hand me your knife, Rick."

Nilwirth reached in back of his neck and withdrew a double-edged knife with a six-inch blade that came to a needle point and looked razor-sharp. He handed it to Websterby who took it and ran his thumb gently along the edge of the blade.

"It'll do," he said. "You two hold the girl."

Looking down at me, he said, "I'll tell you what I'm going to do to her unless you tell me where the old man is. First, I'm going to cut up her pretty face. You'd like that, wouldn't you, girlie? Then I'm going to work on the rest of her. By the time I'm through with her even Luke won't want her."

He reached over suddenly and grabbed Annabelle by her hair, at the same time flicking the knife in and out. She screamed and as he let go I could see a trace of blood on her neck where the knife had barely broken skin.

"That was just a hint, Tackett," he said. "The next time it'll be the real thing."

"She's fainted, Boss," Nilwirth said.

"Get some water and toss it on her," Websterby ordered von Cart.

He turned to me again. "It's up to you. Annabelle and me have all day."

I stared at him and he stared back with the coldest eyes I'd ever seen. He wasn't crazy. He was just mean, cruel mean. He'd do what ever he had to do to get his way and enjoy every minute of it.

"He's hidin' in the brush on the other side of the stream," I said.

CHAPTER 19

I WAS HURTING IN body and in spirit. The agonizing pain in my belly had eased a little, though I'd of been hard put to go for a walk. But the biggest hurt was in my heart. I had betrayed my Pa.

I had betrayed my Pa to save a woman I hardly knew. But whether I knew her or not wouldn't of made no difference. I couldn't let Websterby do to her what he said he'd do. Pa was different. Pa was a man and a tough man at that. He gone through a lot in his days without flinching and he could go through more. Still, I had betrayed him, and nothing would ever change that.

As soon as I'd spoken, Websterby sent his men out to see if they could round up Pa. Even alone, I expected Pa could give them a fight—unless they surprised him. And he wasn't alone. He had Coe and Willie with him, so I wasn't much worried. The four of us waited for something to happen or for Websterby's men to come back, with or without Pa. I kept on sitting there on the floor with my knees pulled up to my chest. The hideout knife strapped to the inside of my left calf was in easy reach, but it wasn't no match for two men with guns so I made no move to get it.

Annabelle sat at the kitchen table dabbing at the knife scratch on her cheek with her handkerchief. She was white as a sheet and every now and then she gave a shuddering sigh. When she looked at me I tried to give her a reassuring smile but no one knew better than me that it was a mighty weak try.

Websterby and von Cart sat at the table with Websterby at the end. Von Cart sat across from Annabelle with his back to me. Both men had drawn their guns and laid them on the table in easy reach.

After a few minutes more the pain begun to let up some and I began concentrating on how to get out of the pickle I was in—and how to do it in time to help Pa. A man who was supposed to be wise once said if a man could concentrate a hundred percent for two minutes, he could solve any problem. Of course, when he said that he wasn't looking down the barrel of a gun. Howsomever, I did the best I could.

Neither man was paying much attention to me so I eased my right hand down the inside of my left leg, covering it with my left hand and arm. I inched my pantleg up above the top of my boot and got my fingers on the haft of my knife. I sat there like that, not moving, waiting for something to happen.

Suddenly there was a burst of firing from the direction of the creek. Both Websterby and von Cart swiveled their heads around to face the sound of the shooting. I never hesitated. I snaked the knife from its sheath and in the same motion threw it at von Cart's back. I didn't wait to see if it stuck him, but launched myself at the table. But Websterby was already reaching for his gun.

He was rattlesnake fast and he beat me to it. As I slid across the top of the table I saw him raise his arm and start to bring it down.

When I came to I was lying on the floor with my arms tied behind me. Through pain-dimmed eyes I could see Pa. He was lying facing me with his arms tied behind him. I knew he wasn't dead because they had him tied up, but he was unconscious and wasn't moving.

"Woke up, I see," Websterby said. "I was afraid I might have hit you too hard."

I raised my head and craned it around so that I could see him. He was sitting across the table where he'd been sitting when I made my run at him. Annabelle was also sitting there, too, along with the two gunmen, Nilwirth and Annen. I didn't see von Cart or the third Websterby hand and then I remembered throwing my knife at von Cart and out of the corner of my eye seeing it stick.

I dropped my head back on the floor without saying anything. "I'm really goin' to enjoy hangin' you and your old man, too," Websterby said. "He'd have been dead a long time ago if I'd had my way. And, as for you, we hang rustlers in this part of the country."

"I ain't no rustler and ya know it," I managed to say between the throbs of pain beating inside of my head.

"Bailey Harbor says you are and that's all I need," he said. "Besides, you killed von Cart and I'll hang you for that if for nothin' else."

So von Cart was dead. Well, I didn't feel too bad about that. I'd given him one chance and I sure never promised him two.

I didn't answer Websterby, but he kept on talking anyway.

"I sent Alex Lamarr to round up the rest of my men up at your old man's ranch. When they get here we'll be goin' back to Kolakoka. I promised Harbor he could watch ya hang and he's still too sore to ride up here."

He chuckled at the thought of Harbor and his burned rear. I would of, too, if my head hadn't been hurting so much, but even so I pictured old Bailey Harbor standing in the stirrups when he climbed on his horse.

"So that old man's your daddy, huh, Tackett?" Websterby asked.

I didn't say anything, just lay there not moving.

"Well, you don't have to answer. I can tell by lookin' at him that you and him are kinfolk. He's not as ugly as you, though, but by the time I'm finished with him he'll be just as dead."

He chuckled again and went on talking, almost like he couldn't stop himself.

"I owe him that. I surely do. He cost me a promotion and damn near got me court martialed. I'd have killed him then if I hadn't been in the army or if I'd thought I could get away with it. I made him sweat all right. For the next two years I made him sweat. Now I'm goin' to make him sweat some more. I'm goin' to let him watch me while I hang you. Then I'm goin' to hang him. I've been waitin' over twenty years for this and I'm goin' to enjoy every minute of it."

I raised my head up. "Seems to me you been carryin' a grudge for a awful long time, Mister."

"Well, I won't be carrying it much longer, boy."

"Ya got my Pa," I said. "What happened to them others?"

"One of 'em's lyin' out there dead. I think it's that fellow, Coe.

The Brown kid took off runnin.' But that doesn't matter much. If he shows up around Kolakoka again we'll grab him. Hang him, too."

"He ain't done ya no harm," I said.

"And he's not ever going to get the chance."

Before he could say anything else the door banged open and the third gunman, the one Websterby called Alex Lamarr, burst into the room.

"I come across the boys afore I ever got to Tackett's ranch," he said and he was chuckling. "They was barefoot and walkin' real slow and careful. Said Tackett here took their boots and horses. I brang Clint Bilton back with me ridin' double. I told him to take some horses and go back and bring 'em in. Don't know what they're gonna do for boots, though."

"You can take a pair off of that dead man out there in the woods," Websterby said. "And von Cart doesn't have any more use for his. And old Honerock's got to have two or three pair lyin' around."

"You leave Uncle Frank's things alone," Annabelle flared, suddenly coming alive in her chair.

"Shut up, girl, or I'll carve your other cheek," Websterby rasped. "Luke, you go on back to the bedroom and round up any boots old Honerock had. Nilwirth, you go get 'em off von Cart and that other dead man."

Annabelle slumped back down and didn't say anything else as the three left the kitchen.

"The boys are goin' to want a piece of you when they come in," Websterby remarked to me casually as Nilwirth and Annen went off to follow his orders.

"Turn me loose and let 'em have at me," I said.

Websterby chuckled. "Now there's a thought. I haven't seen a good fight in a long time. And I've got just the man for you. Name is Fenn Du Bersteen. Nobody's ever beaten him in a fight. Matter of fact, I saw him kill a man with his fists once. I suspect that after you took his horse and boots he'll be wantin' to kill you, too."

"I don't s'pose you'll turn us loose if I whup him?"

Websterby laughed out loud. "No, I don't s'pose."

"How 'bout lettin' Annabelle go, then? She ain't done nothin' to ya."

"Nothin' doin'. I promised her to the men."

I heard a low moan from the direction of Annabelle.

"Hang in there, kid," I said. "It ain't never over 'til it's over."

"It's over, Tackett. It's over," Websterby said. "Take my word for it."

I changed the subject. "What'd ya do to Pa?"

"Nothin'. The boys said his horse shied and threw him when the shootin' started. He hit his head on a rock. He ought to be comin' to pretty quick."

I quit talking and put my head back down on the floor. If I was going to have to fist fight someone I was going to need all my strength to say nothing of a head that wasn't aching too bad.

I closed my eyes and must have dozed off for a minute. When I opened them Pa was looking right at me.

"Howdy, Pa," I said.

"Howdy, son," he replied.

I heard a chair scrape and looked over to where Websterby was sitting. He got to his feet and came over to look down at us.

"I see you're both awake," he said and kicked Pa hard in the back with the toe of a pointed boot.

Pa never made a sound, never even flinched. He was a tough old man, all right.

"You haven't changed any, Websterby," he said. "You're still a brave man when the other fellow can't fight back."

Websterby moved forward to kick him again, but changed his mind. "Talk all you want, Tackett. I've been tellin' your boy what I'm goin' to do. I'm takin' the two of you back to Kolakoka and I'm goin' to let you watch me hang him and then I'm goin' to hang you."

"It's a long way to Kolakoka," Pa said,

"Not far enough for you," Websterby replied and turned and went back to the table.

We must of laid there for another hour waiting for Websterby's men to come in. I kept flexing my hands, trying to keep them supple and keep the blood flowing. If I was going to have to fight the man called Fenn Du Bersteen I at least needed to be able to make a contest of it.

I tried to think of who he might be and finally settled on one of the men we'd captured back at Pa's ranch. He was a bear of man, almost as tall as me and probably weighed fifty pounds more, none of it fat. He had black, greasy hair, a beetle brow and a funny little rosebud of a mouth below a flattened and broken nose. He hadn't said anything when we took his boots and horse, just looked at me with pure hatred in his squinty little black eyes. I'd thought at the time that I wouldn't want to run into him in the dark. Now it looked like I was going to run into him in the broad daylight.

It was well past noon when I heard the sound of horses' hoofs in the yard. "They're back," Websterby said, getting up from the table and going to the door.

Pa and me hadn't had nothing to eat or drink all day, but Websterby forced Annabelle to cook him and Annen and Nilwirth some lunch. When she'd asked if she could feed Pa and me, he said, "Don't bother" and went on chewing on the slice of roast beef he was eating.

Websterby opened the door wide and his men come trooping in, Alex Lamarr and the rest of the men we'd left stranded at the ranch. They were wearing boots that weren't theirs and that in a couple of cases looked to be they were pinching their feet.

"Let's hang 'em now, Boss," one of them said when they saw me.

"Leave 'em alone," Websterby said. "I told Harbor we'd bring them down to Kolakoka so he could watch, and I owe him that. But I have an idea you're goin' to like. Du Bersteen, how'd you like to fist fight young Tackett here?"

"I'll kill him," Du Bersteen growled, glowering down at me.

"That's the one thing you can't do," Websterby said. "We're goin' to hang 'em both, like I said. But I don't care how bad he's hurtin' when we hang him so if you want to beat the livin' hell out of him first why we'll go outside and you can have at him."

"You gonna turn me loose or do I gotta fight him with my hands tied?" I asked, looking up at Websterby.

"Turn him loose," Du Bersteen growled. "It won't do him no good."

"Turn him loose," Websterby ordered. "and get his Pa on his feet. I want him to watch this. Her, too," he added, gesturing at Annabelle.

Annen reached out a big hairy paw, and grabbed Annabelle by the arm. As he yanked her out of her chair she let out a little cry of pain.

I was on my feet by then and Nilwirth had just finished cutting loose the ropes that bound my wrists. I lunged at Annen and caught him with a wild swing along side of his jaw. He staggered backward and only the table saved him from falling. He straightened up and charged, but before he reached me Websterby jumped between us.

"Cut it out!" he hollered.

Annen stopped dead in his tracks. "Later," he said as he glared at me over Websterby's shoulder. "I'll get ya later."

Websterby clapped him on the shoulder. "I'll tell Du Bersteen to save a little of him for you. All right, Tackett, outside," he said, giving me a shove.

I followed Annabelle and Pa out the door, shaking my head a little to see if I could clear some of the haze away and flexing my hands and shoulders to loosen them up. I knew I was in for the fight of my life, even if I'd been been feeling good.

Du Bersteen was already outside and though the air was a mite cool, he'd stripped off his shirt, showing a massive, muscular chest covered with curly black hair. His huge hairy arms were like young oak trees. What neck he had would of done a work horse proud.

Now, like I've said, I'm a big man, and I've got my fair share of muscles from working the mines up in the high sierras and from all the heavy work I've done since. But I felt like a boy standing across from Du Bersteen.

"He's all yours, Fenn. Go get him," Websterby said.

CHAPTER 20

D<small>U</small> B<small>ERSTEEN</small> <small>GAVE</small> a roar that sounded more animal than human and charged at me. I dropped to one knee, meaning to grab him by a leg and flip him over my back, but I acted too quick and he stretched out one leg and leaped at my face. I rolled out of the way but before I could get to my feet he had already turned and was on top of me, flailing away with both fists. I managed to cover my face with one arm, but even so he landed a clubbing right on my left temple that made me see stars.

He was sitting higher on me that he should have been, and I flang my legs up, got them in front of his face and brought them back down again, bending him over backwards. He rolled off of me and we both scrambled to our feet. We circled each other breathing hard, but all of a sudden I felt good. My head wasn't throbbing any more and my muscles, cramped and stiff from being tied all that while, were loosening up.

He charged me again and I stuck out a straight left hand to ward him off but it didn't work. He grabbed it with both of his huge hands, turned his back on me, and threw me over his shoulders— with what I'd heard they call a "flying mare." I landed flat on my back and all the air whooshed out of me. Du Bersteen reached down and grabbed me by my hair and yanked me to my feet. He pulled me in close, wrapped his arms around me, lifted me off my feet, and began squeezing. I knew in a minute he was going break my back and there was nothing I could do about it. I was helpless.

Then I heard Websterby shout, "Don't kill him, Fenn! Don't kill him!"

He dropped me, and I crumpled to the ground like a sack of potatoes.

As I lay there trying to catch my breath Du Bersteen turned away from me. I heard him say, "He ain't much of a fighter, Boss. What do ya want me to do with him?"

"Work him over a little more," Websterby said, "Then Nilworth can finish up. But remember, I don't want you killin' him. We're still goin' to take him back to Kolakoka and hang him with his old man."

Du Bersteen turned back to me and thinking I was worse off than I was, aimed a kick at my belly. In desperation I reached out, grabbed his foot with both hands, and twisted it with all my strength. I heard something snap and at the same time Du Bersteen screamed and fell to the ground, with me still holding onto his foot. I gave it another twist, putting all my weight into it, and Du Bersteen screamed again.

I let go and got slowly to my feet, leaving Du Bersteen writhing and groaning on the ground, clutching at his right knee.

I looked at Websterby. "Ya know what they say. In fightin', the legs go first."

He glared at me. "I should have let him kill you. A couple of you men help Fenn into the house. Someone else go find that doctor."

Before he could say anything more, a man shoved his way through the circle of people who'd been watching the fight.

"What's goin' on here?" he demanded.

It was Sheriff Alecks.

"Nothin' that's any concern of yours, Sheriff," Websterby said. "This is a private matter."

"Not in my town it ain't."

"These are all my men, Sheriff," Websterby said, waving his hand at the small crowd. "All but these Sacketts, here."

"Tacketts," I corrected automatically.

Websterby ignored me. "And we're takin' them back to Kolakoka with us and we're goin' to hang them there and if you make a fuss we'll take you, too."

"See here," Alecks blustered. "You can't—"

He stopped in the middle of his sentence as one of Websterby's men jabbed him hard in the back with a six-shooter.

"You want 'em, you can have' em," he said, shrugging his shoulders. "But ya oughta get out of here today, before the townsfolk get all riled up. This was a pretty quiet town until you fellers come along and they pay me to keep it that way."

"No sense in creatin' a stir," Websterby said. "So I'll tell you what I'm goin' to do. I'm goin' to leave two of my men here with Du Bersteen until he's fit to ride. And to make sure nobody here makes any trouble for them, I'm goin' to take the little lady here with us. I'll send her back when the boys get back to the ranch."

"Dammit, man, you can't—" Alecks began. But he stopped again when the man with the six-shooter prodded him in the back one more time.

"Shall I kill him, Boss?" the man asked, and I saw Alecks flinch.

"Nah," Websterby said. "He's not goin' to give us any trouble. Are you, Sheriff?"

Alecks shook his head. "You fellers go ahead and take care of things here. I got other things to do."

Websterby chuckled. "They can wait, Sheriff. I'd appreciate it if you'd stay here until we're ready to go. In fact, it might be a good idea if you were to go with us a ways. In the meantime let me have your gun for safe-keeping."

The man who had gone to find Doc Marien came hurrying up. "I found the doc in the saloon, but he wasn't drunk yet. Too early, I guess. Anyways, he went after his bag and said he be right here."

Websterby turned to me. "I'll take care of you later," he said grimly. "One of you men tie him up again, and the girl, too. Put them in the barn so the doc doesn't see them. Then get their horses ready. We'll be pullin' out of here as soon as the doc takes a look at Du Bersteen. Oh, yeah. Leave the girl alone for now."

Annen taken his six-shooter out and herded Pa and Annabelle and me into the barn and closed the door behind us. He shoved Pa against the wall of the barn and told him to sit down. Then he came over to me and spit in my face.

"That's for starters," he sneered.

He handed Annabelle a length of rope and ordered her to tie my hands behind my back. I thought about trying to make a break for it then, but decided it would be a stupid trick—even for me. The fact was, I was so weak from the beatings I'd taken I could hardly stand, and my head was throbbing like someone was beating on it with a hammer.

After Annabelle tied my hands, Annen walked around in front of me again and give me a sudden two-handed shove in the chest. I stumbled back against the wall and slid down beside Pa. Then he had Annabelle tie my right leg tight to Pa's left leg. Wasn't any way Pa and me was going get up, tied the way we were. And for sure we wasn't going run in any three-legged race.

When Annabelle had us tied, Annen grabbed her and pulled her to him. "You and me are gonna have a good time later on, little honey," he said. "I got first claim on you." He dragged her over to the barn's center post and quickly tied her to it. "Don't go anywheres, little honey. I'll be back," he leered and stomped out.

"You all right, Annabelle?" I called, looking over at her, but she didn't answer. She'd fainted. All Pa and me could do was sit there and hope she'd be all right. In a few minutes she came to and lifted up her head. It was dim in the barn and I couldn't see her eyes but when I spoke to her she didn't answer, just sat there and stared straight ahead.

For the first time I heard Pa curse. He spoke in a low tone but it made me glad I wasn't one of those on his enemies list, especially Tod Websterby.

After a bit he stopped and I asked, "Pa, what is it between you and Websterby? Why do ya hate him more than other Yankees?"

"It goes back to my time as a prisoner of war, son. I told you how I served under General John Hunt Morgan. Well, back in the summer of '63 we raided clear up into Indiana and Ohio.

"We rode nearly a thousand miles that summer, son, before they finally ran us down and captured what was left of us. When they did, they refused to recognize us as prisoners of war and treated us as common criminals. They shipped Morgan and his remaining officers—sixty-five of us—to a state prison in Ohio.

"They sent a small group of Union officers and enlisted men, including Tod Websterby, who was a major like me, to supervise the prison and the prison guards. Websterby was a cruel and arrogant officer even then, without a shred of charity or human kindness. I told you about the hole they put me in. There's nothing Websterby can do to me today that can equal that.

"After I spent thirty days in that tiny iron cell for helping the General and those others escape, I got sent back down again as punishment for standing up to Websterby. I can't tell you how horrible it was to go back a second time, after being there once and watching men go mad and die.

"The war ended in the spring of '65, but it was a year later before they turned us loose. I was among the last to go and by that time Websterby had been transferred and, I guess, mustered out.

"I had no way of tracking him down or I would have killed him then. You have learned in the last few days how truly evil he is. I cannot allow that kind of evil to exist, son. I am going to have to kill that man."

I looked at Pa and I could see he meant it. Reliving his time in the prison had got him all worked up. There was anger and more in his voice and after he quit talking he kept biting his lips out of rage and frustration.

"First thing we got to do is get loose, Pa," I said gently.

"We will, son. We will. I can feel it in my bones."

I didn't say nothing, but I thought maybe the fall on his head had addled his brain a mite. Just to make him feel better I said, "One thing sure, Pa, we're going to do our dangdest."

We sat there for a long time not talking and then the barn door opened and Websterby and Nilwirth came in.

"Damn you, Tackett," Websterby said, glowering down at me. "You ruined my best man. You twisted Dub's knee clear out of its socket. That doctor says he'll never bend that knee again. I have a good notion to do the same to you before I hang you."

Without warning he stomped down hard on my left knee. In spite of myself I couldn't help letting out a low groan of pain.

"There'll be more later," he said. "Come on, Nilwirth, let's get these people mounted. I want to make some miles by dark."

Nilwirth cut the ropes that bound me to Pa and yanked both of us roughly to our feet. Websterby untied Annabelle but she just sat there looking straight ahead.

"Get up," he said, nudging her with his foot to get her attention. She never moved. He reached down and pulled her to her feet. She stood there dumbly, looking straight ahead. Websterby slapped her face twice but she made no sound or motion. Finally he took her arm and marched her out of the barn while Nilwirth followed, pushing Pa and me ahead of him.

Most of Websterby's men were mounted and ready to go. I noticed with some satisfaction that we'd whittled their number down to five, not counting him and the two men who were staying with Du Bersteen. On our part we'd lost Guy Coe, a man I'd hardly got to know, but a good man from what I'd seen of him.

Even though Annabelle was wearing a dress, Nilwirth picked her up like she was a feather and threw her astride a man's saddle.

"You can't do that," Alecks protested. "You can't treat a lady like that."

Without hardly looking Websterby backhanded him across the face. "You don't have any say in this, Sheriff," he snarled. "Not if you're plannin' on comin' back to Cutbank. Get these two in the saddle, boys."

A moment later Pa and me were mounted, still with our arms tied. Nilwirth took ropes and tied one around my neck and one around Pa's. He tied the end of one to his saddle horn and Annen did the same with the other.

"Just want the two of you to get used to the feel of a rope around your neck," Websterby sneered.

Annabelle, her dress riding up around her thighs was sitting silently in her saddle, holding on to the horn with both hands and with her head bowed on her breast. She was all but unconscious.

Websterby took a look at her and swore under his breath. "Sheriff," he ordered, "you ride alongside the girl and make sure she doesn't fall out of the saddle."

He touched his spurs lightly to his horse and led us out of the yard and toward the trail heading south to Kolakoka.

CHAPTER 21

OUT OF CUTBANK, Websterby took us on the trail leading south. If we rode steady it would take at least two full days to get to Kolakoka—two days longer for me and Pa to live, two more days to plot our escape. Trouble was we couldn't do much plotting because they made sure to keep us apart.

It was late afternoon before we'd got started and in less than two hours, just after the sun set, Websterby led us off the trail and into a long strip of woods bordering both sides of a stream.

"We'll stop here for the night," he said, dismounting.

I climbed stiffly off of Old Dobbin, sore in every muscle and joint. My back was stiff from the squeezing I'd taken from Du Bersteen, and my head was pounding in great dull thuds. I staggered as I got both feet on the ground but Annen was holding the other end of the rope around my neck and he yanked on it, half choking me but keeping me from falling.

I looked over at Pa and he was holding up good for an old man, only I could see he was pale under his tan and there were big dark circles under his eyes. He had to be hurting from his fall earlier in the day. Furthermore, we neither one of us had had anything to eat or drink since morning. My tongue felt like a wad of cotton and my belly felt like it was pushing against my backbone. But at least I was still alive and I had the satisfaction of knowing I come close to destroying Todd Websterby's bully boy, Fenn Du Bersteen. At least he would never walk normal again. I would savor that for as long as I lived, even if it turned out to be only two days.

I watched Sheriff Alecks dismount and lift Annabelle down from her horse. Cradling her in his arms, he carried her over to a grassy spot and laid her on the ground. Annen, standing nearby, sneered, "She ain't much of a woman, is she?"

Alecks clamped his lips together, and without saying a word took off his jacket, covered Annabelle's shoulders and sat down beside her. I hadn't thought much of him at the beginning but I was thinking better of him now. It was plain he was in love with Annabelle and he was doing his dangdest to protect her in a situation where protection was near impossible.

They tied Pa and me to separate trees and tied our hands in front of us, I guess so we could feed ourselves. One of the men started a fire and it wasn't long before I could smell coffee boiling and bacon frying.

Annen walked over to me with a tin cup filled with water. "Boss says to give ya a drink," he said and threw it in my face. I didn't say anything and he laughed and walked away, not knowing that the water on my bruised and battered face felt good. He came back in a minute with another cupful. This time he handed it to me. I taken it in both my bound hands and sipped it slowly, letting it cool my mouth and soak into my tongue. The water was from the stream and it tasted sweet and good.

One of the other men brought Pa a drink and after he finished it he gave a big sigh of relief.

That was all they gave us, just the water. They never even looked our way while they ate. But I'd gone hungry before and I knew if I lived that I would again. I noticed they let Alecks eat with them, and while Annabelle shook her head at the food she sipped at some hot coffee.

It was dark before Websterby and his men finished eating. Websterby told two of them to stand guard and the rest begun laying out their bedrolls in preparation for turning in. The two standing guard took up posts at the edges of the camp and on opposite sides of it.

Websterby was restless, and he wandered over and looked down at me. He was fiddling with a knife that looked to have about a six-inch blade. I was sure it was mine and that Websterby taken it from von Cart's back.

"This is quite a knife," he said, running his left thumb along the edge. He drew it back with an oath and stuck it in his mouth. He sucked on it a moment and then took it out and spit on the ground. "Damn thing is sharp as a razor," he said, inspecting the thumb. "I cut myself pretty good."

I didn't say anything, but then he asked, "Where'd you get it?"

"Off a broke sailor in San Pedro, out in California," I said. "He told me he got it from a Gypsy man whose life he saved. I ain't never seen a piece of steel like it; it don't never rust."

"Interestin'," he said. "I'll just hang onto it since you won't be needin' it."

He stuck his thumb in his mouth again and walked back to the campfire. He squatted there a few minutes, talking in low tones to the two men who hadn't turned in. Then he strolled over to where Alecks was sitting by Annabelle who seemed to be sleeping.

"I don't want to have to tie you up, Sheriff," I heard him say. "But I will if you even think about leavin'. Besides, you leave and you'll never see that girl again. Hear?"

"I ain't goin' 'less I take Miss Annabelle with me," Alecks said.

"Just so long as we understand each other," Websterby said, walking away. He bedded down on the other side of the fire and pretty soon the others turned in, too.

Pa was too far away for me to try to talk to him without others hearing, so I leaned back and dozed off.

One time the guard on my side of the camp came over to Pa and me and checked our bonds, but he was wasting his time. We'd been tied by someone who knew what he was doing and there wasn't no way we were going to untie ourselves.

The night was halfway gone when they changed the guard. The men who'd been on watch come in and built up the fire again but it wasn't long before they went to their bedrolls.

I dozed off again and this time neither one of the guards bothered to come around and check on us.

I was sitting there half asleep and half awake when a voice behind me whispered, "Tackett."

I sat up straight and as I did I felt the rope that was binding me to the tree fall away. At the same time a strong arm pulled me to my feet and a knife slashed the ropes that bound my hands.

"We go now," Whitewater said softly.

"Pa?" I whispered. "What about Pa."

"I'm here, son," he whispered.

"We go," Whitewater said urgently.

He and Pa moved through the trees like ghosts and I followed as quiet as I could. We walked beside the stream for a few minutes and then at a spot that was barely a yard wide, Whitewater stepped across it and led us over a low hill and into a small valley, probably no more than a mile from where Websterby was camped.

There were two small fires burning and a group of men were sitting around them. When we came up close, I saw that most of them, about a dozen, were Indians. Zell and Clara Botrish were there, too, and so was Willie.

There wasn't no squaws in the party.

Two of the Indians came over and began talking to Whitewater and Pa in Sioux. One was Eagle Beak. The other one, I learned later, was his brother, a warrior named Darting Snail. I was suprised to hear Pa join in the conversation. Somewhere in his wanderings he'd learned the language.

Whilst they were talking I went over to Zell Botrish. "Thought you was headed for Helena," I said.

"Clara and me figured you couldn't get out of trouble by yerselves so we found Eagle Beak and his people and they agreed to give us a hand, so a bunch of us headed back this way. Next thing I knowed, Whitewater showed up with Willie here and told us you was captured and everyone else was dead so we come to see if we could turn ya loose."

"Willie was only part right," I said. "They kilt Coe but Pa was only knocked out and they captured him, too. They was takin' us back to Kolakoka where they was meanin' to hang the both of us."

"That would have been a terrible thing," Clara said. "It would have made me a widow before we were even married."

"You can marry Willie here," I said. "That way you can be his wife and his Ma both."

"I ain't marryin' no injun," Willie burst out.

Just then Pa and Whitewater and Eagle Beak walked up.

"We'll eat first," Pa said. "Then we'll talk."

They had venison and some kind of meal they made by crushing acorns and Botrish cooked up some frying pan bread and made some coffee. That was the best part—the coffee. It was black as sin and hot as Hades but after what Pa and me had been through it tasted good, real good.

"Son, we're going to put an end to this now," Pa said gravely as we sat sipping our coffee. "Eagle Beak and his Indians are going back to Websterby's camp with us. We're going to surround it and at daybreak we'll attack. Son, those are evil men there and we mean to take no prisoners."

"What about Annabelle and the sheriff?" I asked.

"We'll try to save them," he said, but it didn't sound to me like saving the two of them was all that important to him.

"Pa," I said, "ya can't do this. If we can capture 'em we got to do that. Dang it, Pa! We ain't no murderers, you and me. Neither is Zell here nor Willie. If we can capture 'em, then we can take 'em back to Cutbank and the sheriff can hold 'em for trial."

"Those are evil men, son," Pa repeated stubbornly, and I saw a kind of crazy gleam in his eye.

"Yer lettin' yer hate for Websterby get in the way of yer thinkin'," I said. "Ya can't make them injuns and the rest of us part of yer hate."

"As long as those men live, wherever they are, decent men and women can't be safe," Pa argued.

"I won't be part of it, Pa," I said hoarsely. "I ain't never kilt a man in cold blood and I ain't gonna start now. You do what ya gotta do but me and Old Dobbin'll be hittin' the trail. Willie, too, if he wants to come. And anyone else."

Pa and me stared at each other for a long moment, and then I turned away. I remembered suddenly that Websterby still had all our horses, including Old Dobbin, and I almost changed my mind.

No, I told myself. I ain't no bushwhacker. I ain't no murderer. If I have to I can always get me another horse.

Pa's voice behind me said, "Hold on a minute, son. How do you want to go about this?"

A great feeling of relief swept over me. It sounded like Pa had come to his senses.

"Surround the camp, like you said. But come daybreak holler out for 'em to surrender. If they don't then we start shootin'. But, Pa, we just can't murder 'em in cold blood no matter what Websterby ever done to you."

"I'll talk to the Indians," Pa said.

He walked over to where Whitewater and Eagle Beak and Darting Snail were waiting. They talked among themselves for several minutes, then Pa came back to me.

"We'll do it your way, Del, but if any one of Websterby's men goes for a gun then we'll begin shooting."

"You won't never be sorry, Pa," I said softly.

We moved out with Whitewater and Eagle Beak leading the way for the Indians and the rest of us following. When we got near the camp, Eagle Beak held up his hand for us to stop, then gave a signal and the Indian braves disappeared in the brush and the trees. In a few minutes an owl hooted from the other side of the camp and then another answered.

"Lot of owls out tonight," Willie said.

"Them ain't owls, Willie," I replied.

The five of us—Pa and me and the Botrishes and Willie—moved up to where we could see the light of the Websterby campfire. We were all armed. Willie and Botrish each had an extra six-shooter in their bedrolls and they'd lent them to Pa and me.

A cold dawn wind sent a shiver through me and I thought how lucky we were that the snow we'd expected had missed us. Not that I was a stranger to snow. Up in the sierras where I was raised I've seen it six feet deep and deeper. But I was hoping to be back in Arizona before winter hit. I didn't relish the idea of being trapped in Montana 'til spring, which always comes late up there.

It was beginning to get light and I could see a stirring in the camp as men began crawling out of their bedrolls. The two guards strolled toward the fire from opposite sides of the camp, then suddenly Pa shot off his gun.

The bullet hit the campfire and scattered sparks and ashes.

"Websterby," Pa called. "You're surrounded. Surrender now and you won't be hurt."

Inside the camp men began diving for cover and a hail of bullets clipped the trees around us. Pa yelled "Fire," but the Indians were already firing and so were Willie and Botrish.

In the dim light I saw Sheriff Alecks throw his body on top of Annabelle to protect her.

It was all over almost before it began.

"Don't shoot, I surrender," one man shouted and stood up. An Indian bullet caught him in the body and he staggered backward and fell in a heap.

"We surrender!" The voice crying out was Websterby's. "Don't shoot."

Someone, I suspected it was Eagle Beak, shouted something in Sioux and the shooting stopped.

Pa called out, "All you men stand up, throw down your guns, and put your hands on your heads. Anyone there tries anything and you're all dead.

"Alecks! You and Annabelle get over here."

We waited 'til Alecks half led, half carried Annabelle to where we were lying. Clara got up right away and took the other girl in her arms.

"You'll be all right now," she crooned. "You'll be all right now."

Pa stood up and shouted out something in Sioux. From all around the camp, the Indians moved in—all except Whitewater who, as usual, was nowhere to be seen.

Pa walked toward the captured men with me and Zell and Willie right behind. There were four men standing, including Websterby, and two on the ground. One of them, Luke Annen, was dead. I didn't know the wounded man by name, but I recognized him as one we had captured at Pa's ranch.

Tod Websterby stood there, hands on his head, his face contorted with rage and hatred.

"Damn that Bailey Harbor," he snarled at Pa. "If it hadn't been for him I would have killed the both of you back in Cutbank and let him watch me hang Botrish or that kid Willie when we got back to Kolakoka."

"Yer a nice man, Websterby," I said.

Pa walked up close to him. "Websterby," he said in a low tone that I could barely hear, "after I got out of your hell hole of a prison I swore that if I ever ran into you again I would kill you. If I had known you were in Montana, I would have run you down and killed you a long time ago.

"If it hadn't been for Del here you'd be dead now. It was him who kept me from having you and your men slaughtered, which is what I wanted to do. But he's not going to keep me from killing you now. Like Del said, I'm no murderer, so I'm going to kill you in a fair fight. How do you want it? Knives or guns?"

"Neither one, Tackett," Websterby sneered, "You're mistaken if you think you're goin' to kill me. I don't fight vermin like you. I hire people to do that."

"You'll fight me, Websterby, or I'll kill you where you stand."

"There are witnesses here, Tackett. If you kill me you'll have to kill everyone here. Otherwise you'll hang. It won't be me who hangs you, but you'll hang."

As I watched, Pa grabbed him by the front of his flannel shirt, pulled him up close, and flang him down on the ground. Websterby sprawled onto the dirt and laid where he had fallen, glaring up at Pa.

Pa spit in his general direction and turned away. As he did I saw Websterby sit up and reach into his boot. He pulled out a knife and drew his arm back to throw it.

All in the same motion, I drew my gun and fired. I saw what looked to be a chunk of Websterby's skull fly off. He never made a sound, just fell back on the sod, the unthrown knife dropping from his hand. His feet kicked a couple of times, his body twitched, and then he was still. I looked again and half his head was blown away.

Pa had whirled and hit the ground at the sound of the shot. When he saw me standing there with the smoking gun in my hand he slowly got to his feet.

"He was gonna knife ya, Pa," I said, holstering my gun.

I walked over and picked up Websterby's knife—only it wasn't his knife, it was mine, the one he'd kept after he took it out of von Cart's back.

I wiped the blade on my jeans, pulled up my pantleg, and stuck the knife back in its sheath.

Pa stood looking down at his old enemy. "He was mine," he said. "I'm sorry he made you do that."

"Better me than you, Pa," I said, putting my arm around him.

"I guess you're right, son," he said.

We made Websterby's men bury the dead where they lay. Then we bound them and mounted them on their horses which Willie and Zell had saddled.

Eagle Beak and Darting Snail had a long talk with Pa and the Botrishes, which I couldn't understand but I could see Clara shaking her head and figured she was telling them she wouldn't go back with them to the tribe. At the end the Indians came around and shaken hands with us, white-man fashion. Then they mounted and rode off toward the south where their camp was.

Annabelle was pale and shaky, but she had finally come out of her stupor and Alecks had jury-rigged a side-saddle so's she could return to Cutbank riding like a lady.

Herding Websterby's remaining men ahead of us we trotted into Cutbank just before noon. The few townspeople on the street stopped and stared as we dismounted in front of the jail and ordered our prisoners inside. Alecks rounded up two loitering cowboys and deputized them to guard the jail whilst he taken Annabelle home and went and fetched Doc Marien.

The five of us—the Botrishes, Willie, and Pa and me—walked down to the town cafe, pulled two tables together and ordered coffee. The waitress said, "The cook just finished making doughnuts," so I ordered out a dozen and we sat there sipping coffee, dunking doughnuts, and talking about what we would do next.

"Bear sign is what they used to call doughnuts," Pa said. "That was when they fried the centers instead of the outsides."

"What are you going to do now, Del," Clara asked, and I thought there was kind of a wistful tone to her voice.

I looked at her. She was a pretty girl, dark, with black hair and eyes, good regular features, and even white teeth. But she wasn't for me and we both knew it.

"There's a girl waitin' for me down Arizona way," I said. "I'm headin' that way and I'm hopin' Pa'll come along."

"I can't son," Pa said. "There's the ranch and the cattle."

My heart sank. "Pa," I said, "after all these years I can't lose ya now. Come down to Arizona with me now and you and me'll come back in the spring, round up yer cows and drive 'em to market or to Arizona, whatever you say."

"I'll think on it, son," Pa said, taking a bite of doughnut.

"Willie, yer welcome to come along, too," I said.

"Been thinkin' about it," Willie said. "I'm goin' back to Kolakoka. Mr. Botrish is still the depity there and he aims to run for sheriff now that Websterby and von Cart are dead. He says he can use a depity."

"There is a school there, too," Clara said. "There are the children of white men and the children of Indians to be taught. They need a teacher there more than they do in Helena so I've decided to stay with Father. Besides," she added. "Willie's still young enough to need a mother, especially since he says he ain't never gonna marry a injun."

"Aww," is all Willie said, turning red and scratching at a pimple.

"Whyn't we lay over here until tomorrow, get us some rest today, see that Miss Annabelle's all right and pull out of here first thing in the mornin'?" I suggested. "By that time Pa'll know what he wants to do."

Pa, who had been sitting silent while the rest of us talked, looked over at me. "I've made up my mind, son. I'm going with you. Family is more important than cattle. Besides, I want to be there when your wife has my first grandson."

CHAPTER 22

WE STAYED AN extra day in Cutbank for Frank Honerock's funeral, and the whole town turned out for it. Annabelle held up well considering what she'd been through and never strayed from Sheriff Alecks' side.

Strange how things work out, I thought. A few days ago she couldn't stand him. Now he was dang near her idol. Well, that was all right. He might be a lot older than she was and and might not have the proper upbringing, no more than I had, but he loved her and would of given his life for her. No doubt in my mind, he'd make her a good husband.

We left Cutbank on good terms with the sheriff, who thanked us for our help and dropped the charges against me for slugging him in the head.

"I'm hopin' Miss Annabelle will marry me," he confided to Pa and me. "Now that her uncle's dead she needs a good man to care for her. Her and me would make a great team. She can run that newspaper her uncle left her and I'll uphold the law.

"Come back and see us," he shouted after us as we rode out of town.

We rode steady for two days and on the morning of the third we trotted into Kolakoka and reined up at the jail. Zell Botrish had pinned his badge back on and he waved to townsfolk he saw on the street.

"This is a good town," he said. "You sure you don't want to stay on a while?"

"They tried to hang me here," I said drily. "I think Pa and me'll have some breakfast. Then we'll be movin' on."

He told us where the cafe was and we said goodbye to him and Clara and Willie.

"I'll come visit ya sometime," Willie said, blinking back a tear.

"Yer a good man, Willie," I said. "You can ride the trail with me anytime."

We started to shake hands but then I reached out and taken him in a bear hug.

"Don't be a stranger, hear?" I said, pushing him away.

"You don't have to go, you know," Clara said softly.

"I got to go," I said, a tiny part of me wishing that I didn't.

She stood on her tiptoes and kissed me lightly on the lips.

"You needum squaw, you come back to Kolakoka," she whispered and ran into the jail.

"Like I always said, injuns are notional," Botrish said, grinning. "She'll get over ya. You two ride careful and come back anytime."

Pa and me mounted up and rode over to the main street and tied our horses in front of the Main Line Cafe.

"We have fresh eggs," the waitress said.

"And bacon?" Pa asked.

"And bacon," she smiled.

We both of us had four fried eggs and about half a pound of bacon each, along with toast and wild honey and steaming hot coffee. Then Pa surprised me. When we were drinking a third cup of coffee he reached into a leather pouch he wore strapped to his belt and got out two small cigars which he had carefully wrapped in a piece of oiled silk.

"My last two," he said. "I've been saving them for a special occasion and this is it."

We licked them good to keep the tobacco leaf from coming loose, bit off the ends and lit up. There is nothing like a cigar after a good meal and we sat there for a while puffing away.

"Time to go, Pa," I said.

I paid the bill, gave the waitress a dime for her good service, and we walked out the door.

"Tackett," a low, mean voice said.

Pa and I turned together to face it and it was Bailey Harbor.

"I been waitin' for ya ever since word come you was on yer way here. Now I'm gonna kill ya," he said, and he had a gun pointed at my belly.

"Dang it, Harbor! Go away and leave me be," I said. "I don't want to fight ya. Yer boss is dead and there ain't no reason for you and me to fight."

"I ain't gonna fight ya, I'm gonna kill ya." he said and there was cruel satisfaction in his voice, "In fact, I'm gonna kill the both of ya."

"You leave Pa outa this," I said, "and I'll fight ya fair, guns or knives or fists."

"Only fools fight fair," he sneered. "Yer dead meat, the two of ya."

I saw his finger begin to tighten on the trigger and I threw myself hard to one side. Out of the corner of my eye I saw Pa do the same thing, and both of us were going for our guns.

But there wasn't no gunshot from the direction of Bailey Harbor, only a terrible, anguished scream.

I looked up at him and he stood there pawing uselessly at the sharp, pointed end of what looked like the point of a knife blade jutting out of the front of his chest.

His gun dropped into the dusty street and he screamed again and again. Then he crumpled and fell on his face and I could see the haft of an army bayonet sticking out from his back. Twenty feet behind him and to one side, still standing where he had thrown the bayonet, stood Chief Whitewater. He walked up, put his foot on Harbor's back, and pulled the bayonet free. He wiped the blade on the back of Harbor's vest and slid it carefully into the sheath he wore slung over his left shoulder.

"You save my life, I save yours," he said to Pa. Then he turned and walked away.

"He dang sure saved both our lives," I said. "What's this all about anyway, Pa? It's more than just him likin' white folks."

Pa nodded. "When he first came into the country around Cutbank he took sick one winter. I found him in his cabin nearly dead.

He had no food or firewood. He was half-starved and nearly freezing. I bundled him up and took him to the ranch and nursed him back to health. He lived with me all that winter and in the spring he just walked away.

"But, like I told you, I've seen him from time to time over the years. Sometimes he'll come by the ranch and stay a week. Every now and then he'll bring half a deer or an antelope that he's killed. I may be the nearest thing he's got to a real friend."

"Lucky for us," I said as a crowd began to gather.

Zell Botrish came elbowing his way throught the crowd with Willie at his heels.

"My God! What happened?" he asked when he saw the body. Leaning down he turned it over. "Bailey Harbor! Well I am damned! Who done this?"

"He was meanin' to kill Pa and me," I answered him. "He didn't reckon on Chief Whitewater."

"I didn't hear any shots," Botrish said.

"He throwed his bayonet at him. It went clean through him."

"Where's he at now?"

"Gone," Pa said. "And, Deputy, if you have no further use for us, Del and I will be going, too."

"You'll like it in Arizona," I said to Pa as we cantered out of town. "I've got me a girl there and a big black dog and a snootful of friends. Besides, it's a lot warmer than Montana in the winter time."